ALL MY HAIRY BITS

The full 'Wax and Whips' Trilogy

...or How NOT to date!

First Published in 2020 Copyright © 2020 S J Carmine. All rights reserved. This is a work of fiction. Names, characters, places, and incidents are products of the author's imagination or are used fictitiously and should not be construed as real. Any resemblance to actual events, locales, organizations or persons, living or dead, is entirely coincidental. No part of this book may be used or reproduced in any manner whatsoever without written permission, except in the case of brief quotations embodied in critical articles and reviews. All enquiries or comments to reallyreallynovel@gmail.com

Contents:

Book 1

Wax, Whips and My Hairy Bits

Book 2

Shoes, Blues and Erotic To-Do's

Book 3

Flamingos, Fears and Happy Tears

Book 1

WAX, WHIPS AND MY HAIRY BITS

CHAPTER ONE

Me

I used to love reading romance novels, nothing modern, just good old fashioned Victorian romantic literature. It was a time of innocence, the pace of life was slower, the men more charming. A time where you didn't have to conform to female stereotypes online, where you never needed to ask 'does my arse look big in this' because everyone looked big in a bustle and no fucker was going to get a look at your arse until you had a ring on your finger. It gave me hope that there was a Mr Romance out there for us all and then suddenly it dawned on me that actually it was all a little bit dull. It took me a bit of time to realise where it was all going wrong, but then it became clear. These novels, lovely as they were, were missing one vital component…they didn't do cock.

My name is Ann, not regal Anne, just plain, boring, unexciting Ann. I often wonder how my life would have turned out if my parents had just given me that extra 'e'. I am thirty-two years old, no spring chicken and no stranger to the dating scene. I work in marketing which isn't as glamorous as it sounds and if I'm honest it bores the shit out of me. The search for my Mr Romance had led me to a succession of short, infuriating relationships where the sex had been no more exciting than a blow job and a quick shag (missionary position). I needed less Mr Romance and more Mr Uninhibited. I needed excitement, hot wax and a fucking good seeing to. I was single, more than ready to mingle and had read a shit load of Erotica so I knew exactly what I had to do in order to embark on a new sexual adventure. I wanted no strings sex, none of that emotional bollocks, just a good hard fuck and maybe a cup of coffee in the morning. I'm bored of feeling boring. I don't want to be Ann who's a good laugh, I want to be Ann who's amazing in bed, I want to be the shag that stays with you a lifetime, never bettered or forgotten.

My longest relationship had lasted nearly two years, Hayden. We met when we were both at university. I was so young and inexperienced I didn't really know what a good shag was. I lost my virginity to him after four bottles of Diamond White and maybe it was because I was pissed, or maybe because he was shit at shagging, but it was a completely underwhelming experience. There was no earth shaking orgasm, just the feeling something was missing and a sore fanny for a couple of days. We muddled along, foreplay was always the same, I gave him a blow job, he tried to find my clitoris…the man needed a fucking map. Sex was nearly always missionary, I'd sneak on top whenever I could, but he'd always flip me over for a quick finish. Maybe we just became too familiar with each other but when he started to not take his socks off when we had a shag I knew it was time to move on. He wasn't that arsed to be honest, I think he'd started to prefer his games console to me anyway and if he could have stuck his knob in it I'm sure he would have dumped me before I dumped him. My relationship history since Hayden has been unremarkable, hence my decision to ditch the romance novels and dive head long, or should that be muff long, into Erotica.

I'm suppose you could say I'm reasonably pretty and my face is holding up well, which is surprising given my twenty a day smoking habit, absolute love of kebabs and a probable dependency on Prosecco. My tits aren't too bad, they measure in at a 36C and I'm pleased to say they are still nice and perky and probably a few years off resembling a Spaniel's ears. My legs are long and shapely and the cellulite on my arse can be hidden with a good, supportive pair of knickers. Thongs just aren't going to happen, sorry Erotica but negotiating with a piece of cheese wire up my arse does not do it for me whatsoever. I've been researching my subject well recently, and one of the first rules when embarking on an erotic adventure seems to be that one must have a shaven haven, a freshly mown lawn, a smooth muff…I think you get the picture. I need to think carefully about how I am going to achieve my erotica ready fanny as the expression 'bearded clam' doesn't describe the half of it!

I don't fancy having my fanny flaps waxed and shaving isn't really an option as I'm petrified I'll get a shaving rash. So the only option I've got is hair remover cream. A quick trip to the shops and it's mission accomplished; my lady garden is smothered in intimate hair remover cream. It looks like a Mr Whippy with sprinkles but definitely no chocolate flake. It's not the most attractive look in the world, I'm staggering around like a saddle sore old cowboy, but it's going to be worth it…I am Ann without an 'e' and without pubes, a bald fannied paragon of sexual liberation. That bird with the posh name in 50 shades of whatever is going to have nothing on me! Though I have to admit, the undercarriage was a bit of a nightmare and to be honest it does sting a bit. At least I don't have to wait too long and then I will be smooth, shiny and....ouch...I'm fucking burning now! Burning is not right surely? Jesus, my flaps are on fire. Give me a minute I need to jump in the shower and get this shit off.

I just spent four fucking hours in A&E. I washed the cream off and my minge was glowing red and burning like a bastard which was almost bearable until the swelling started. I could feel my lips starting to throb, they were pulsating like a rare steak. I didn't want to look down, but I knew I had to…fuck me I had testicles, just call me Johnny Big Bollocks because that is what I had. I quickly checked Dr Google and the best thing for swelling is elevation and an ice pack, so I spent the best part of half an hour with my minge in the air and a packet of frozen peas clamped between my thighs. Needless to say it had no effect at all and it became painfully clear that I was going to have to haul my now damp, swollen crotch to the hospital. Never before have I felt so humiliated, having to describe in intimate detail my problem to little Miss Smug Bitch at reception;

'So, you've come to A&E today because your vagina is swollen'...

…well it's my vulva actually but let's not split pubic hairs, or try and get them off with cunting hair remover cream. Sour face huffed and puffed and eventually booked me in, I spent what felt like an eternity pacing around…I couldn't sit down, my testicles wouldn't allow it and by this time a ball bra wouldn't have gone amiss. The Doctor I saw, who was absolutely gorgeous (the one time I didn't want to show an attractive man my fanny) and, when he wasn't stifling a laugh, couldn't have been more sympathetic. I'd had an allergic reaction and he'd prescribe me some anti-histamines which would bring the swelling down, my labia would return to their normal size and other than some skin sensitivity for a few days I would be fine but under no circumstances was I to use hair remover cream again as next time the reaction could be even worse. Though what could be worse than the whopping set of bollocks I'd grown I don't know. So that's that, I'm going to have to go au natural. Which is fine by me, I'd rather have a hairy beaver than an angry one.

A few hours later and my muff has more or less returned to normal and other than feeling slightly itchy seems to be perfectly fine. I've crossed shaven haven off my to do list and need to carry on with my preparation. As you may have already gathered, I've got a lot of work to do. I've noticed in most of the Erotica I've read that the words penis and vagina are rarely used, so I need to practise my sexual vocabulary, I need to learn how to talk dirty…I need to do my Erotica homework. I've had another flick through some of my books and there's no way I can call my vagina 'my sex' I know strictly speaking it is, but for fuck's sake…'my sex craves you', 'my sex needs your sex' it's all sounds a bit contrived if you ask me so I think I'll check out the Urban Dictionary.

I've just spent a good hour trawling through and my God

what an education that was. Either I'm more wet behind the ears than I thought I was or some of the things I've just read are made up, check out 'Angry Pirate'…that's not for real, is it? I'm ready to try some of the new words and phrases I've learnt. I need to be all pouty lipped and doe eyed as I look in the mirror, moisten my lips and purr:

'I want to suck your length'

'Do you want to drink out of my cream bucket'

'My clit is hard and ready to be licked'

'My vagina is the most magical place in the world, come inside'

What the fuck was I thinking, I can't say this shit! Firstly the doe eyed, pouty lip thing makes me look like I'm pissed and secondly I can't do this without laughing. I'm much more comfortable with 'do you fancy a pint of Guinness and a quick shag'. I quickly give my head a wobble, comfortable is boring. I'm in this for the excitement and the clit tingling thrill (see I did learn something). Maybe I'll just opt for quiet and mysterious, let my body do the talking and my mouth do the sucking (I'm really starting to get this now). So that's the plan, my persona will be a sultry erotic goddess who doesn't say much, I'll be irresistible, a fabulous shag who doesn't want a conversation, no chat just sex.

The last part of my preparation is what on earth am I

going to wear? If I'm going for the mysterious look does that mean I'm going to have to channel my inner sex goddess, or does it mean I go for a prim and proper, hair up, professional look? Maybe a combination of both, tight fitting dress, hair up and glasses, then I can do the whole taking my glasses off and flicking my hair down thing. The hair flicking thing however is a bit of an issue for me: my hair is naturally curly…really curly, at university my nickname was 'pube head' which probably tells you all you need to know, so I'm going to have to straighten it to within an inch of its life. From frump to fox…check me out. Today is going to be an exciting day. I'm just waiting for the postman to arrive, I've ordered some proper lingerie. I've gone for two sets initially, traditional black and racy red. Shit, should I have ordered a dildo? I forgot about a fucking dildo and candles, I forgot candles! What about a butt plug…what actually is a butt plug? I can't be erotic if I'm not dripping hot wax on him whilst pleasuring myself with a multi speed vibrating dildo…okay, so maybe not at the same time but you get my drift. Handcuffs! Shit, I'm not very good at this, he'll just have to tie me up with my big knickers.

The postman came, and I swear he had a knowing glint in his eye when he asked me to sign for my delivery or maybe he just read the label on the back of the parcel, cheeky bastard. It took me a while to build up the courage but here I am, standing in front of a full length mirror wearing a bright red, lacy push up bra, matching arse covering comfortable pants, a suspender belt and black stockings. I'm not sure. My tits are standing to attention and look like boiled eggs in a frilly egg cup, they are virtually dangling from my ear lobes and I swear you can see my minge stubble.   So the new plan will be to go for subdued or even better, no lighting at all. I think it's all starting to look really erotic… bushy fanny, no filthy talking and everything done in the dark. The scene is set and I'm ready to get out there. No strings, erotic sex here I come. Well, not quite, I need to sign up to a dating site.

I take a selfie of myself looking as sultry as possible (not doe eyed or pouty, we know that doesn't work) I decide to show a little bit of cleavage and a little bit of leg, but not too much I want to leave my potential dates gagging to see more…I'm such a temptress.   I've written and rewritten my profile about twenty times, it has to be just right and I think on my twenty first attempt I've finally done it:

'Flirty thirty two year old,

 I work in marketing,

I like to get my head down in both the boardroom and the bedroom,

I'm looking for no strings attached fun,

Hobbies include reading, cooking and amateur dramatics.'

I know, you don't have to tell me, it's painfully shit. Hopefully they'll just look at my profile picture and to be honest at this point I don't care, I've submitted everything and I am now a fully paid up member of a dating site.

It takes a couple of hours for my phone to eventually ping with a notification that I have a message, I'm trembling with excitement as I open it...

'You've got nice tits'

Fuck me, 'You've got nice tits' is that it? I mean it's nice he thinks I've got nice tits, but I was expecting a little bit more. No, hang on he's sent a picture...it's a dick! He's sent me a picture of his dick, eww I don't think I've ever seen such a stumpy little penis, it's got a hugely bulbous bellend which looks like it's going to explode at any minute and hang on, it looks like it's winking at me...I'm never going to be able to unsee that! I quickly delete the message, when my phone pings again...It's another dick, not the same dick, this one is long, thin and veiny as fuck. Maybe I'm being too fussy, knobs aren't supposed to be attractive are they? My phone is quickly becoming a rogues gallery of ugly shlongs. I'm really starting to think maybe this wasn't a good idea, I know I said I wanted plenty of cock, but this wasn't exactly what I meant. Three cocks later and just as I am about to give up on the whole idea (maybe a pint of Guinness and a quick shag isn't too bad after all) I get a message from Daniel. I check out his profile and he actually looks quite fit, he's good looking, athletic and he didn't send me a dick pic.

I've been chatting to Daniel over the past few days and I have to admit he sounds lovely, we seem to have quite a bit in common but I can't get carried away by our shared love of ABBA. I'm after a filthy, lustful shag, nothing more nothing less. I'm happy for him to make me come and then go. Next time he calls, I'm going to ask if he fancies going on a date, wish me luck!

Yes! He actually said yes, I am officially going on a date. Once it actually sinks in that I have a date, I start to panic. What am I going to wear, where are we going to go, will I be able to straighten my hair enough to flick it flirtatiously, how much muff stubble am I going to have?

CHAPTER TWO

Daniel

Today's the day! I'm meeting Daniel tonight at the Petite Restaurant…he suggested it and believe me it's well posh. I've never been before but its renowned for being frequented by the upper echelons of society, fuck…It's going to be really expensive. I need to go and extend my overdraft.

Overdraft extended and I'm currently relaxing in a hot bath, my legs and armpits are shaved and are as smooth as a babies bottom, my muff however is as prickly as the bitch receptionist at A&E. My hair is being deep conditioned and I'm wearing a tightening face mask, I've buffed and exfoliated to the point you could eat your dinner off my thighs, I am going to look fucking irresistible, Dan the man is in for the night of his life.

Three hours until we meet. I've painted my nails, my hair is straightened and I've slathered myself in expensive body cream. I wonder what he's going to be like, will we get on, what are going to talk about? What if he's nothing like his profile picture, what if he's short, fat and balding, you hear about this sort of thing all the time…shit I need to think of an excuse to get out of there quickly if I need to:

'I'm sorry Daniel, but I'm going to have to cut this short, I've left the iron on'

'I'm so sorry Daniel, I'm going to have to go my dog will be missing me'

Not sure either of those sound particularly convincing, but it's something to work with. I'm sure it's all going to be fine…and breathe. Time is passing really quickly so I suppose I'd better get dressed, I don't want to be late for the delectable Daniel.

I'm done, dressed up to the nines, looking sultry, sexy and totally up for it. These fucking suspenders are a bit a of nightmare though, I think I've done something wrong as I keep having to pull my stockings up, I probably should have tightened them up…shit, I have so much to learn when it comes to looking, acting and being erotic. Not to worry, I'll stay seated as much as possible and with any luck I won't be wearing them for too long! I pop a packet of condoms in my bag and I'm ready to go.

The taxi pulls up outside the restaurant and I try and get out as elegantly as possible. I wobble slightly on my stiletto heels, I normally wear flat shoes so I'm lacking in high heel practise, why didn't I practise when I had the chance, now I'm going to worried about falling arse over tit all evening. I compose myself and walk in to the restaurant where I am immediately greeted by the maitre d' ;

'Good evening Madam, do you have a reservation with us this evening'

Shit, fuck, do I?

'It's ok Marcel, she's with me'

I turn around and there he is…Daniel, he has the voice of an angel, is as fit as fuck and on first name terms with the maitre d'.

'Hi Ann, lovely to meet you finally'

He's so polite and did I say how fit he was, he is tall, lean, has the most amazing blue eyes and a hypnotic smile. I manage to mumble a greeting and when he tells me I look beautiful, I can feel myself starting to blush. Marcel takes us to our table, Daniel is the ultimate gentleman pulling out my chair and making sure I am seated before him. I take a look at the menu and to my horror, it's in French, I haven't got a fucking clue, my GCSE French knowledge doesn't extend past ordering a toasted ham sandwich.

'Would you like me to order for you?'

Too fucking right I would, I accept gracefully and Daniel

orders for us both. I don't know how often he comes here but he must be a regular as we've just been given a complimentary bottle of champagne. We start to chat and he is such a good catch, I'm beginning to think he's marriage material. He works in banking, volunteers for the local food bank and has a passion for animal charities…twenty minutes in and I think I'm in love.

    The starter arrives and its oysters, good that he has chosen an aphrodisiac and shit because I've never eaten an oyster before. They literally look like fannies, how am I supposed to eat something that looks like my muff? Daniel picks one up, he masterfully squeezes lemon juice onto it (I hope he doesn't do that to me later) and then I swear before he swallows it, he teases it with his tongue…I never thought I'd want to be an oyster, but right now that's what I'm aspiring to. I decide to follow his lead, come on Ann without and 'e', you can do this girl. I try not to look as I squeeze a little lemon onto an oyster, I close my eyes and tip it into my mouth…shit, shit, shit, it's disgusting, It's sitting at the back of my throat like mucus and doesn't want to go down, I swear I'm going to vomit. With one all mighty gulp it slides down the back of my throat, not wanting to look like an oyster virgin I manage to utter a few words;

    'Mmmm, that was delicious, but I'll just have the one as I

need too leave room for the main course'

Daniel deep throated the rest of the oysters, which set my fanny tingling I can tell you. I hadn't even been with him a hour and I was well up for it. If he could devour oysters like that just imagine what he was going to do to my fanny, I bet he would have no problem finding my clitoris.

The main course arrived and it was completely normal steak dish, I wolfed it down as I was starving having passed on the oysters. The champagne is flowing and we are getting on really well, he's so warm and funny. He keeps touching my hand and I'm sure he just brushed his leg against mine. The champagne is going down a little too well and I'm starting to feel a bit pissed. I'm trying my best to be flirty and sophisticated but I can feel my stockings starting to fall down and my muff stubble is itching like I've been bitten by a thousand ants. I excuse myself and pop to the loo to readjust my stockings and have a fucking good scratch.

I get back to the table and desert has arrived, it's the most divine looking chocolate creation I have ever seen, bollocks to the sex, give me more chocolate pudding or even better lets smother each other in chocolate pudding and lick it off…I put this in my mental to do list. We seem to flirt endlessly when it comes to order coffee, I just have to ask the killer question…

'Would you like to come back to mine'

Oh my God, not only did he say yes, but he also insisted on paying the bill…result! We get into a taxi and he puts his hand on my knee, he's touching me, surely that means I'm in. I put my hand on his and can feel electricity course throughout my body…well I say my body but I actually mean my fanny, it is literally pulsating. The taxi stops and we get out, I no sooner open my front door than he pushes me against the wall and kisses me with such passion it takes my breath away. We stumble into my bedroom shedding clothes as we go, Christ he's stunning. I undo the buttons on his shirt as he unzips my dress. I step out of it, hope he doesn't notice my baggy stockings and ask him to wait whilst I light the scented candle by my bed (I couldn't believe my luck when I managed to find one in my local corner shop). So here we are, semi naked in candle light, he unclips my bra, cupping my breasts in his hands, I gasp as he delicately sucks on my nipple and his hand gently rubs my crotch, his fingers brush gently against my clit and I want them inside me. I unzip his trousers and he removes them, he also takes off his socks which is a relief I can tell you. We fall onto the bed, he is rubbing my clit harder now, he finally inserts a couple of fingers and I moan with pleasure. I start to move my hand up and down his shaft and before I suck his cock I decide to emulate the Erotica I have read and drip hot wax on him, I tell him to stop and pick up the candle. He looks excited, I know I am! I straddle him and start dripping wax on his beautiful bare chest. He groans with pleasure as the drops of hot wax hit, I'm really doing it, I'm living my erotic dream and then I don't know what happened, I think I must have too much champagne or snag my baggy stockings but I lose my balance and as I fall I spill molten wax all over his bell end.

Daniel screamed in shock and pain, I screamed in utter mortification. He jumped off the bed and my first instinct was to grab the glass of water on my bedside table and plunge his dick into it. I swear there is steam coming off it as his penis hits the water, the wax hardens as it hits the water and his poor helmet is now dark blue and scented. The cold water seems to help, but he's clearly not happy;

'Fuck, fuck, fuck, what have you done to me, what kind of a fucking candle was that?'

It was the kind of candle you get from the corner shop at the last minute when you are trying to set an erotic scene, how was I supposed to know it didn't meet British safety standards. I gently suggest we get dressed and get him checked out at A&E, I remembered watching a programme about burns so I run to the kitchen and bring back a roll of cling film, I attempt to wrap his penis in it, but he obviously didn't see the same programme as he's looking at me like I've completely lost the plot, if he didn't think I was mad before, he does now. There's not much conversation in the taxi to the hospital, I don't know what to say, what can I say?

'I'm so sorry I've destroyed your bell end.'

'They can do wonders with plastic surgery these days.'

I look at the pained expression on his face and decide that silence is golden. When we arrive at A&E (without cling film) it's just my luck that it's Little Miss Smug Bitch on reception again;

'So you've come to A&E today because you've accidentally burnt your partner's penis with hot wax.'

Well, strictly speaking he's not my partner, but yes I've managed to burn his penis with unfeasibly hot wax whilst emulating an erotic scene I'd read in a book…that turned out well. After waiting for a very uncomfortable couple of hours, Daniel finally manages to get to see a doctor…the same doctor I saw with my minge testicles, I'm mortified and he looks even more gorgeous than he did last time. He gives me a knowing look and again is very professional but is definitely trying not to laugh as I describe how in the throes of my very own sexual adventure I slipped, snagged my baggy stockings and spilt molten wax all over Daniel's penis. I feel like a one woman expose on the funniest things doctors have seen in A&E.

Daniel has superficial burns to the knob, a busted bell end and it's all my fault. Thankfully there's going to be no lasting damage except to his pride. Apparently I did exactly the right thing by plunging his dick into cold water, that should earn me a little forgiveness, surely? I try to apologise, he's very polite and he doesn't blame me, it's just one of those things, a bizarre and unexpected accident, but he doesn't think it would be a good idea for us to see each other again. So that's that then, mission not accomplished. No hot shag, just an incredibly hot dick, only not in the way I was expecting. I help Daniel limp to the taxi rank, and after a polite goodbye and a handshake we go our separate ways. This is not how I imagined the evening ending, the taxi driver asked if I'd had a good night, so I shot him my 'mind your own fucking business you twat' look, which really wasn't fair as he was only trying to be nice. The sun is coming up as a finally get home, what a complete and utter disaster. I need to get some sleep so I can forget about what has just happened, at least for a few hours and I really need to get these stupid suspenders and stockings off.

I've got a raging hangover, my head is banging and I feel crushingly disappointed. Daniel was perfect, the full package. He was all my romantic and erotic fantasies rolled into one. I would have sacked off my one night of dirty sex rule for him, he was a prospect, who knows where we could have ended up…it certainly shouldn't have been A&E. I check my phone and he's blocked me on all his social media, I can hardly blame him. I'll forever be that bird who mangled his manhood. I'm not surprised he doesn't want reminding, the poor bastard is probably going to need therapy after this. My phone pings and I look at it in the hope he's changed his mind and wants to see me again once his burns have healed. I should be so lucky, it's another random dick pic, I can't be bothered scrutinizing it, if it hasn't got a wax coated bell end I'm not interested. I decide to stay in bed and eat chocolate for the rest of the day. I'm destined for blandness, I'm going to be forever vanilla. I finally get up and I'm mooching around the house when my phone pings again, if its another dick pic, that's it I'm giving up and I'd gladly never see another penis again.

I was pleasantly surprised when I eventually looked at my phone, I'd been contacted by Josh who had seen my profile and was interested in exchanging messages and maybe meeting up. He's very pleasing on the eye and I might just be back in the market to see another penis again, maybe, eventually…as soon as possible! So maybe all is not lost and I can continue my erotic adventure, don't call me Vanilla, call me Scarlett…but with no candles or anything combustible whatsoever.

CHAPTER THREE

Josh

I've been speaking to Josh for the past few days and we've got quite a lot in common. He's a couple of years younger than me and his sister was in my year at school. If I'm honest I really didn't like her, she was one of the 'mean girls' and with my sensible shoes and braces I was always a target of her mockery. I'll be totally honest, she was a complete fucking bitch who made my life a misery. But it's not her brother's fault and he doesn't seem all that keen on her either. I think I do vaguely remember him, he was a bit of a Mummy's boy and his Mum always used to meet him at the school gates, which was a bit odd considering he was in year 9 at the time. This was in complete contrast to his sister who didn't need anyone except her fawning group of mates…yes I am bitter and twisted! Today we are meeting up, he suggested a picnic in our local park. He told me not to bring anything, he's going to sort it all…fit as fuck and a gentleman! Before you start, I know it's a bit fucking vanilla, but after my last experience I surely deserve a bit of romance.

It's a beautiful sunny day so I decide to opt for a floaty

summer dress which shows a little bit of cleavage but covers my legs, I'm also wearing flat shoes which is a blessing. I'm just having a pleasant day out with a friend with a view to eventually showing him what a dirty bitch I can be. In the looks department Josh is the complete opposite to Daniel, he's olive skinned with beautiful dark brown eyes and the most amazing thick brown hair…I bet he wouldn't complain about a bit of wax on his bellend.

I arrive at the park and my stomach flips with excitement as I see Josh walking towards me, he looks even better in the flesh and appears to be carrying a proper, grown up wicker picnic basket. I give him a flirty little wave and try not to look to desperate;

'Yoo hoo, Josh'

Shit, did I really just shout yoo hoo! I need to keep calm, maintain my aloof and sexy exterior, fucking 'yoo hoo' what was I thinking. Thankfully he smiles and strides purposely towards me. After my over excited greeting faux pas I wouldn't have blamed him if he'd turned round and walked off. He kisses me gently on both cheeks (how very continental) and my fanny starts to tingle. We stroll for a bit, chatting like we've known each other for years and find a nice quiet spot to have our picnic. Josh opens up his picnic basket and throws a large tartan blanket on the ground for us to sit on, he reaches into the basket;

'I hope you enjoy the food Ann, my Mum was up until midnight making it'

His Mum made the picnic? That's a bit weird - but it does look delicious: ham and salad sandwiches, homemade coleslaw, sausage rolls and lots of chocolate cake. He opens a bottle of chilled white wine and we start to eat. The food is delicious and I am quite literally stuffing my face. We talk and talk, discussing everything from our school days and the people we both remember to our jobs. Josh works in administration and is between jobs at the moment, he's thinking about starting his own business and whilst he sorts himself out he is back living with his Mum, who appears to do everything for him. He talks about his Mum quite a lot, but that's nice isn't it, he obviously appreciates everything she does for him. Feeling stuffed and a little bit pissed from day time drinking, I lie back on the blanket and feel the warm sun on my face. Josh leans over and gently kisses me on the lips…fuck me, I wasn't expecting that but it was very nice! I respond and before long we are having a full on snog in the middle of the park, I'm wet and he's hard but there's fuck all we can do about it. A group of teenagers ride past us on their bikes, 'look at them, they're having a shag'…if fucking only! We come up for air and Josh invites me to have a meal at his house tomorrow night.

I can't quite believe how well today went, I really like him and I really want to fuck him. I spend the evening fantasising about what I want to do to him and what I want him to do to me…where's that fucking dildo when you need one. I know I said this about Daniel, but I think I could be willing to relax my one dirty shag and no ties rule with Josh.

Tonight's the night, I'm nearly ready for my evening with Josh, I'm wearing a figure, hugging, cleavage enhancing little black dress and I've gone for black lingerie to match (no suspenders and stockings, I can't be arsed pulling them up every five minutes whilst I wait for him to pull them down) and I'm pleased to report my muff is looking less like a hedgehog as each day passes. I'm really excited, I wonder what he is going to cook, he did message me to ask if I like chicken, so I'm assuming we'll be having chicken for our main course and I'll be having cock for dessert.

I arrive bang on 8 o'clock and knock on the door, I feel sick with nerves as it slowly creaks open…hang on, that's not Josh it's his;

'Mother, I'm Josh's Mother, Sylvia, and you must be Ann, do come in'

Josh is waiting for me in the hall, he kisses me tenderly on the cheek and I would say my fanny is tingling but his

Mother is watching, it's a bit unnerving if I'm honest. I can feel her looking me up and down, it's like she's taking mental notes. I get the feeling she's already made her mind up about me and she's not keen. I can smell the food cooking and it really does smell delicious, Josh must have been in the kitchen all day, bless him. We go into the dining room and Josh pours me a glass of white wine, there must be some sort of mistake as there are three places set at the table.

'I hope you don't mind but Mum is joining us for dinner, she's been cooking all day so I couldn't say no when she asked'

Now this is really fucking strange, his Mum is eating with us, his Mum has cooked dinner, his Mum made the picnic when we met at the park. I thought Josh was cooking dinner, I thought Josh was going to arrange our picnic, but it's all been his Mother. I take a breath and put it out of my mind, she's clearly just being a lovely Mum, helping her son impress his potential girlfriend…yes that's it, totally not odd at all. We take our seats as his Mum serves the first course, it's a beautiful homemade cream of spinach soup with croutons no less. I tell her how wonderful the soup is and try to make polite conversation but she keeps staring at me, a really deep, intense stare like she's trying to look into my soul. Josh puts his hand on my knee, I can't fucking react because Starey Mary has me right in her sights. As he's stroking my leg I notice he's looking at my tits, I can see the lust in his eyes, he's absolutely gagging for it.

Sylvia notices him ogling me, she looks really pissed off and without a word gets up and goes into another room, she returns carrying a heavy woollen shawl which she drapes around my shoulders completely covering my magnificent cleavage 'I thought you looked a little cold' she snarls. I do my best to look appreciative but I'm seriously starting to freak out a bit. She doesn't sit down and clears away the bowls, when she leaves the room Josh apologizes and explains that since his Dad left them she's become a little bit possessive of him…not just a little bit mate! We can hear her crashing about in the kitchen, plates are clattering and she slamming doors furiously. Something tells me she's not thrilled about me being there. Sylvia brings in our main course, it's a traditional roast chicken dinner. She slams my plate down in front of me and just as I'm about to take my first mouthful the questions start;

'What do your parents do?'

'How many boyfriends have you had?'

'When do you intend on having children, you're well past your prime?'

Well past my prime, cheeky bitch! I try and answer as

honestly and politely as I can, except I dodge the boyfriend question I'm not telling her that, she can fuck right off. I need a quick break so I ask if I can use the loo, as I walk upstairs I notice all the pictures on the wall, they are all of Josh and his Mum, it's like the rest of the family don't exist. I'm beginning to understand why his sister was so much of a bitch. I have pee, reapply my lipstick and head back downstairs, on the way down I can hear Sylvia talking, I don't catch much of it but I definitely hear her say…

'She's not right for you Joshy, her love pillows were hanging out. She's a slut'

Joshy? slut? Love pillows? I am literally chewing my cheeks with rage when I walk back into the room, I don't want to spoil the evening but where does the wizened old hag get off calling me a slut…chance would be a fine thing. Bless him, Josh looks at me awkwardly, this must be so embarrassing for him so I decide not to say anything. Thankfully we've managed to get to pudding without Sylvia asking any more difficult questions, I compliment her on how good her trifle is and she barely acknowledges me. She glares at me as she clears the table, she's watching my every move and I wonder what is going to happen next, I don't have to wait too long. She get's up abruptly, slamming her chair under the table;

'Goodnight Josh, I'm going to bed, goodnight Ann it was nice to have met you'

Fanfuckingtastic, the witch has gone to bed and its finally just me an Josh. I was starting to think she was going to sit with us until I was forced to leave because it was so fucking uncomfortable. We have another glass of wine and when he's convinced Sylvia is out of the way for the evening, he silently takes me by the hand and leads me to his bedroom. His room is immaculate with nothing out of place, to my horror on the wall is an almost life sized picture of Josh and Sylvia, fuck me she's going to be watching everything. I decide not to look at it, I can't look at it…shit this is weird. Josh soon takes my mind off it as he tenderly strokes my hair and starts to kiss my neck, my hairs stand on end, this is really happening! I feel him breathe gently into my ear as he says;

'Fuck Strumpet.'

What the actual fuck? I push his head away and ask him what the hell was that?

'Tonight, you're my Fuck Strumpet.'

'No, Josh I am many things, but Fuck Strumpet?..come on, call me something else!'

He starts to kiss my neck again, my fanny is pounding with desire, I'm hot, moist and ready to go. I feel his hot breath in my ear again as he calls me;

'Mummy.'

You have got to be joking, he didn't really just call me Mummy? He fucking did, he doesn't want a girlfriend or a Fuck Strumpet, he wants a Mummy substitute. He wants another Sylvia, Sylvia the second, mad bitch troll from hell mark two… That's it, I need to get out of here, I quickly think of the excuses I had practised in my head and without thinking I tell him I have to leave;

'I'm sorry Josh, err I have to go. My dog needs me!'

Josh looks bemused as I head towards the door, I explain that I have a psychic connection with my dog and I can just feel he is distressed and needs me to go home right now, this minute, without delay…I don't actually have a dog, but that's not the point. The point is I need to get home and away from this weirdness. I grab my bag, open his bedroom door and fuck me, Sylvia is standing right in front of me, if looks could kill I'd be six feet under and she'd be dancing on my grave. How long has she been there, and if I wasn't leaving would she have been there listening whilst I gave him a blow job, would she have walked in whilst we were having a shag? I bet she'd drilled a peep hole into the door or set up hidden cameras. My imagination starts to run away with me and I'm seriously starting to fear for my safety, the woman is like something out of a horror film, as I push past her I hear Josh calling my name followed by Sylvia calling me a slut, but I'm not looking back as I open the front door and run full pelt towards the nearest taxi rank.

Well that was another monumental disaster. I didn't even get past first base, didn't shed an item of clothing or get within lusting distance of his cock. Josh has been non stop messaging me, he wants to know if I'm ok, if my dog is ok...what the fuck do I say?

'My imaginary dog is fine but your Mother is a psychopath.'

'You called me Mummy...and your Mother was listening at the door.'

'You seriously need to cut the cord, sweetie.'

I decided on a quick 'it's not you, it's me' message, I'm sure Sylvia will make him a comforting hot chocolate, tell him what a lucky escape he's had from the evil slut bitch from hell and tuck him into bed. I think I need to read some more Erotica, because this is not going how I planned. I'm not exactly the heroine at the moment but her sad mate who never gets anything right, I must admit I'm starting to think I might be better off looking for steady, reliable, BORING Mr Romance, as Mr Uninhibited seems to be somewhat difficult to pin down. Maybe I'm just not cut out for sexual excitement, maybe I'm destined for a life of wham bam thank you, Mam.

I'm just dropping of to sleep when my phone pings, really? I'm not sure I can be fucking arsed to be honest. I leave it until my curiosity gets the better of me. I open the message and to my surprise it's not a dick pic. It's a message from Spencer, he's 34 years old, a lawyer who enjoys classic comedy and lists horse riding as one of his hobbies…judging by his profile picture, he can ride me anytime!

I decide to let him stew and respond in the morning, maybe that's what I need to do, make myself less available, be more mysterious and aloof.

After a good nights sleep I respond to the delectable Spencer. There's no messing about with this one, he got straight to the point and invited me to meet him at one of the best hotels in town. I'm supposed to be meeting up with the girls this weekend but I'm sure they'll understand when I explain just how hot he is, I can't let them down, can I? I've got to go for it, Spencer could be a once in a lifetime fuck or maybe even a keeper. I'll just check if I can extend my overdraft again and then I'll let him know.

CHAPTER FOUR

Spencer

Tonight's the night I'm meeting Spencer. I'm so excited I could explode, the girls were a bit miffed I was letting them down but when I showed them his picture and told them where he was taking me they totally understood. They've made me promise to tell them everything, they want to know all the gory details, hopefully there's going to a lot to talk about. I think they are starting to feel sorry for me after my last two disaster dates, I don't want to be the friend they pity because she's not getting any, I want to be the friend they come to get top fanny tingling tips.

Spencer and I have been messaging a lot over the past few days, he wants to know everything about me which is a good sign. Hang on, he's just sent me another;

'How do you feel about BDSM?'

BDSM? I haven't really got an opinion, I've never heard of them if I'm honest, they sound like a heavy rock band which really isn't my thing. They're probably American and come to think of it, I'm sure I saw someone wearing a BDSM t-shirt once so they must be quite popular. I don't want to show my ignorance so I'd better do some research before I get back to him, it would be awful if he starts to talk about his favourite band and I haven't got a clue who they are. I google BDSM…what the fuck! Bondage, dominance and whoa this is full on Erotica. What do I say;

'I'm more a missionary type girl myself but I'll give anything a go.'

'I'll gladly give it a try but there's no way I'm wearing a gimp mask.'

'My thighs are too big for PVC.'

I decide not to reveal my naivety and tell him I love of a bit of BDSM…he responds by telling me tonight he's going to be my Master…what the fuck have I done! I put it out of my mind as I get ready, I'm pleased to report my muff stubble has grown and now resembles a neatly trimmed bush, I've ditched the stockings and suspenders so he'll have to make do with smooth, fake tanned legs. I decide to try out my stiletto heels again tonight, if he's into BDSM he'll probably want me to keep them on. I'll need to pack a bag for tonight, but what do I put in it? I don't own anything remotely resembling a negligee and I'm guessing he's not a fluffy pyjamas kind of guy. I'll just pack the basics and tell him I always sleep naked…how very erotic of me!

Spencer is waiting outside when I arrive at the hotel, he's even better looking than his picture and I feel like I'm punching above my weight. He's not as tall as I thought, but he's muscular as fuck. His pecs are straining against his shirt and I can see the muscles in his thighs bulging against his trousers. I suck in my stomach and head towards him. We exchange pleasantries and as we walk into the hotel he gives my arse a cheeky slap, I don't quite know how to react so I just give him a knowing smile. He takes me up to our room so I can drop my bag off before dinner. We get into the lift and I'm not sure what to say to break that awful 'we've just met for the first time' silence, I decide to say nothing, I'll maintain my air of mystery and just look sultry. The lift judders to a halt, the doors open and I follow Spencer out, as I step out of the lift I trip slightly on my heels but manage to regain my composure without him noticing.

The room is amazing and to be honest, its less of a room and more of a suite. I'm like an excited child as I check out each room and I can't help myself I just have to sit on the huge double bed and have a bounce. Spencer looks bemused, I think he's wondering what he's let himself in for. As we head out of the door I make a mental note to take home the complimentary toiletries, some of the flavoured coffee sachets and the luxury cookies.

We go down to dinner and I although I try hard not to, I start to think about Daniel, I'm pleased to say there were no candles in our room so I won't be repeating the events of the night of which I never speak. Spencer orders a bottle of champagne and we start to talk. We actually get on really well and have lots in common, he's very charming and extremely intelligent. You can tell he's a lawyer, he asks gentle, probing questions, nothing too heavy but enough to get all the information he needs out of me. Just as I'm starting to feel comfortable he comes out with a killer question;

'So Ann, tell me, what was your most exciting sexual experience'

Oh fuck, what do I say?

'Well this one time I managed a whole 2 minutes on top before he flipped me back into the missionary position.'

'I had a quick shag in the toilets in the Student Union!'

'I dripped hot wax all over this bloke's bell end!'

I'm starting to sweat as I try and think of something to say which is not going to out me as an Erotica virgin, when suddenly I'm inspired…'I thought someone like you would know Spencer, a lady never tells'. He gives me a knowing look, he either thinks I'm a real goer or he's sussed that I lack experience in some areas of my sexual education. I think that did the trick because as the evening goes on we become more and more flirtatious, he touches my hand as he talks to me and I've taken to flicking my hair coquettishly. He's excellent company and very funny, I'm giggling like a schoolgirl every time he opens his mouth. We finish our meal and he insists on paying the bill, I might not be getting much sex in my quest for sexual enlightenment but I'm certainly eating well!

We have another couple of drinks at the bar and Spencer asks if I fancy heading up to our room…too fucking right I do! We get into the lift and as soon as the doors shut Spencer kisses me, a full on, passionate, fanny tingling snog…I'm up for anything now, Erotica, BDSM…bring it on! He puts his hand between my legs, moves my knickers out of the way and inserts a finger…fuck me I'm being fingered in a lift…this is a first. Maybe tonight is the night I'm going to get more than a quick clit tickle and a finger job. We get into our room and the sexual tension is palpable, he kisses me again, devouring me with his tongue, I am literally putty in his incredibly experienced hands. He undresses me slowly, savouring every moment, until I am standing in front of him completely naked apart from my stiletto heels…I knew he'd like the shoes.

'You really are beautiful Ann'

That's it, he's got me now. He's staring at my muff and I'm walking down the aisle. He's checking out my tits and

I'm thinking of baby names. I saunter towards him (please don't let me trip) confident, sexy, like I know what I'm doing, but my lack of experience means I'm playing this all by ear. I unbutton his shirt as he puts his hand between my legs and gently teases me again, fuck me my fanny is tingling, I'm hot, wet and gagging for it. I can't concentrate and fumble with the buttons, it would be so but much easier if I could just rip his shirt off, but it looks really expensive. I undo his belt and pull his trousers down, his erect cock is standing to attention and I really want to give it some! I have to resist the temptation to suck it there and then…play it cool Ann, play it cool. He pulls me towards him and kisses me again, he starts to play with my nipples and as I feel his dick rub against my pubes I'm struggling to contain myself, I just want me inside me…NOW! I need to calm myself down, this is what I've been building up to, hot, erotic sex not a quick fuck.

'Get on the bed Ann'

Here we go, what's he got in mind, I'm assuming he's going to want some sort of foreplay and if he wants to lick my clit I'm not going to say no. He's being very assertive, well he did say he was going to be my Master tonight. I lie down trying to recall some of the erotic 'come and fuck me now' bed scenes I have read, I throw my head back, arch my back and I open my legs slightly.

'No, don't lie down, get on your hands and knees'

Get on my what now? This is getting very erotic, I am actually doing it, finally I'm going to have exciting sex. So what's he thinking, is he going to go in from behind, I don't mind starting off with a bit of doggy style…I'm ready and waiting Spencer. He walks behind me and I'm starting to feel a little bit self- conscious, can he see my cellulite? Are my tits hanging down too low? Is there anything on the bottom of my shoes? What is he going to do to me? I have a quick look and see him reach down for something. It's a fucking horse whip…I know, I know its classic Erotica but I'm not sure its classic me. I think Spencer can sense my tension;

'Relax, Ann, you're going to love this, you've been a very naughty girl'

Maybe he's right, I'm open minded and I am being very naughty, this is exactly what I've been working up to…CRACK! He whacks my arse with the whip, maybe I should have told him I don't have a very high pain threshold. I yelp with pain and then I don't know what comes over me. It was such a shock and it fucking hurt, even though I knew it was coming and I should have been prepared…there was nothing remotely pleasurable about it, my fanny isn't tingling and my arse is throbbing. Unfortunately, it triggers some sort of primeval defence mechanism and I leap up, whip around and punch him on the end of the nose. Now he's shouting in pain as his nose appears to explode, there's so much blood, thank goodness he's not wearing his expensive shirt. I've clearly played this all wrong, I should have cried out in pleasure and pain when he whipped me, that's what they do in the books isn't it. But me, no I have to punch him in the face…shit! I run to the bathroom apologising profusely, I bring back copious amounts of toilet roll and he tries to stem the bleeding.

'Ahhhh! You've broken my nose! I think I'm going to have to go to hospital, I thought you were up for this Ann?'

Fucking hell, I can't go back to A&E, can you imagine what Little Miss Smug Bitch would have to say if a roll up there with another Erotica induced injury. I persuade him to see how it goes, noses do bleed a lot…don't they? I try apologising again, it was an automatic reaction because of the shock of the horse whip, and as soon as his nose stops bleeding we can try again. Needless to say Spencer doesn't have much of an appetite for resuming our liaison. I get dressed as he politely tells me it isn't going to work, if he'd known I was so inexperienced he wouldn't have used the horse whip, he thought we were on the same page but clearly we're not. Thankfully his nose has stopped bleeding (it does look a bit swollen though) and we shake hands as I leave. I don't even have the time to fill my bag with the complimentary toiletries or posh coffee...what a fucking travesty. We say a formal goodbye, half an hour ago we were about to have sex and now we are parting like polite strangers. Shit, I forgot he's a lawyer, I hope he doesn't sue me!

I feel like crying as I head home, what the fuck am I doing wrong. So far on my erotic adventure I've burnt a bell end, escaped a psychopathic mother and broken a nose and I still haven't managed to have a shag, the packet of condoms in my bag remains unopen, they're going to go past their sell by date at this rate. Maybe this is a good time to accept my destiny and give up, I'm not cut out for this Erotica shit. I'm tired, pissed off and my arse hurts. I arrive home and go straight to bed, alone again.

My phone is full of messages in the morning, none of them from Spencer just my friends wanting to know what I'd got up to. They all laugh when I tell them what happened and yes, it would have been quite funny if it had happened to someone else. But it happened to me and I'm mortified...again. I'm tempted to message Spencer just to ask how his nose is feeling, but I think better of it. I don't think I could take the humiliation of him telling me to fuck off. I get in the shower and look at my arse, there's a cracking bruise on my right cheek, so that will be a timely reminder for the next few days. Erotica is clearly not for me, I'm just not cut out for it. I've tried and failed spectacularly, I think I'm going to have a break from men for a bit. Maybe I'll get a dog for real, a faithful little companion that doesn't whack you on the arse or set his mother on you.

I spend the rest of the day mooching around, I bag up all my Erotica novels ready to take them to the charity shop, I'm serious, that's me, I'm going to live like a nun for the foreseeable future. Just as I'm considering cancelling my membership of the dating site my phone pings with a message…can I really be arsed looking at it, I leave it for a bit and then have a look. To my surprise it's a message from James. James is forty (a bit older than I'd normally go for), he's divorced (could be tricky if his ex is a bitch) and he is a car salesman (he probably talks a lot of shit). He's nowhere near as good looking as my previous disaster dates, but maybe that's a good thing. I'm not sure whether to respond or not, this whole thing has been such a monumental disaster but then, maybe it could be third time lucky. I send him a quick message back, nothing ventured nothing gained and all that. Shit, where did I put those books, I need to get back to my reading.

CHAPTER FIVE

James

I've been taking it quite slowly with James, we've exchanged messages and spoken on the phone a couple of times. He has a lovely, deep reassuring voice, but he does have a tendency to whisper. I really don't think I'm going to have to worry about whips, wax or weird Mothers with this one. I think I might be ready to meet him, I think I'm ready to carry on with my quest for a fucking good shag.

I leave it another couple of days and then ask James if he would like to meet and today we are meeting at the zoo. I know, I know there's nothing erotic about a trip to the zoo, there was nothing erotic about having a picnic but that ended up quite steamy and who knows where that night would have ended if it wasn't for evil witch Sylvia. I've got to stop thinking about the disasters of the past few weeks and start to look forward optimistically, I've will get it right eventually…won't I?

I meet James at the zoo entrance and he's tall, tanned and not half as good looking as my previous dates, but there is something about him. I can't quite put my finger on it, there's an air of mystery to him. I get the feeling he's going to surprise me. It's not all about looks after all, it's what's inside that matters, there's no point in being with someone who's drop dead gorgeous if they have a bad heart. We start our zoo tour with the big cats, we're fortunate to arrive at feeding time, watching the lioness devouring a huge lump of meat empowers me, take a look at that Jimmy Jogs, that's what I'm going to do to you later…maybe, if I can just start to fancy you, even a little bit. The conversation is flowing nicely and we enjoy the full zoo experience. We feed the giraffes, watch the sealion show and right now we are having a ride on the zoo train…I should be grateful, it's the only bloody thing I've managed to ride successfully.

Taking a break from the excitement of the zoo train we sit beneath a beautiful old willow tree in a quiet piece of woodland, there's no one about which is quite romantic really. He's even bought me an ice cream…what a gentleman. We chat about anything and everything, he was married for ten years and thought he was blissfully happy until his wife had an affair with his twin brother…his twin brother what a fucking bitch! He'd come home from work unexpectedly and caught them mid shag, how do you get over something like that? It had been two years since it happened and he hadn't spoken to his brother since, he tells me how it had torn his family apart. They didn't have any children which was blessing because he wouldn't have wanted them to grow up in a broken home. I knew there was something about him, he's a poor damaged soul, well I might just be the woman to repair him. His divorce recently came through, he's just started dating again and feels like he's a little bit rusty. It's taken him a long time to build up the courage to even think about a new relationship. I tell him he's doing just fine and he should have more confidence in himself. I think he appreciates it as he gives me a little peck on the cheek, does my fanny tingle, not really but there's still time.

We had a lovely day at the zoo and as we part company James promises he'll be in touch, I'm not quite sure what that means, will he really call me or is he sacking me off gently? I did like him, but he just didn't excite me like the others, he was less 'fuck me' and more 'could you get me a nice cup of tea and a slice of cake'. My transformation into an erotic goddess hasn't gone too well so far, so maybe taking it slowly is just what I need at the moment, slow burn and then a crescendo to sexual enlightenment. I've decided I'm going to play it cool and wait for him to contact me, I don't want to look too keen.

It takes three days for James to finally message me, three fucking days. He wants to see me again…well maybe I'll keep him waiting a few days whilst I decide or maybe I'll just give him a quick call. We have a pleasant chat on the phone and arrange to meet at the Dog and Duck pub, not quite as exiting as I would have liked but you never know, there might be a quiz on. At least I don't have to dress up and I really don't think I'm going to need to wear lingerie, so comfortable it is. I decide on jeans and a cleavage enhancing top…let him see what he's missing out on.

When I arrive at the Dog and Duck, James is waiting outside;

'Hey, Ann!'

That was it, just a 'hey'. No kiss on the cheek, not even a handshake…he's not interested is he. We head to the bar and James asks me what I would like to drink, fuck it, I'll have a pint of Guinness. I don't need to pretend I'm a sophisticated exponent of the erotic arts tonight, I think James sees me as a friend, his buddy (but not of the fuck variety), his old china. We take our drinks from the bar and just when I think things can't get any more mundane;

'Quick Ann, we need to find a table before the quiz starts.'

I was joking about the fucking quiz! He finds us the most secluded table in the pub and collects our entry form for the quiz, we don't have a team name, we are simply Ann and

James…how very unexciting, we're like a talent show group that can't be arsed coming up with a band name. I'm sorry James but it's a big no from me. The room falls silent as we wait for the first question:

'What is the oldest recorded town in the UK?'

Before I can think 'I don't have a fucking clue' James has written Colchester. That's impressive…if it's right. This continues question after question, he doesn't need to ask me anything. There's no conferring in this team, the man is a trivia genius. Thirty questions later and James finally comes up for air, he's been so engrossed in the quiz he's barely acknowledged me. I even tried pushing my tits up a bit higher until they are virtually spilling out of my top…nothing. James hands the quiz sheet in and so begins the long wait to see if we've won. Now he doesn't have anything else to think about he's chatting away happily, I think he's starting to feel more comfortable with me as I'm sure he was just looking at my tits. I should give him a chance, he's had his heart broken and he's getting back on the dating horse, though would I want to ride him? I'm still not sure.

'Our winners tonight are…Ann and James!'

We won! Well, James won and the prize?...beer vouchers (how glamourous), hmm...I guess it's a free night out if nothing else. As the alcohol start to flow, so does the conversation. James is actually quite funny, he's definitely got hidden depths and I'm warming to him. He may not be classically handsome but he has a certain something about him, he brushes his leg against mine and yes, I've got a fanny tingle…not an intense one, but at least things are starting to happen. As the night wears on, he moves his chair closer and closer to mine, he's catching my gaze when he talks to me and I'm getting the feeling him might be up for some fun;

'Ann, should we get a bottle of wine to take out and go back to mine?'

I agree and try not to look too keen, maybe tonight's the night I unleash my inner erotic goddess, I'm not fucking dressed for it but that doesn't matter does it? I can still look erotic in my comfy pants, it what's inside that's important! We walk back to James' house and strangely he walks a little bit ahead of me, when we arrive he has a good look around before he opens the front door then literally throws me through, he's either well up for it or has nosey neighbours.

His house is very homely and there are photographs of him and his wife everywhere, the poor man he must still be broken hearted. He takes me through to the sitting room, puts the bottle of wine down on the table and kisses me passionately, well I wasn't expecting that…what's the rush! I respond and decide to take the initiative. I undo the buttons on his jeans and slip my hand inside his boxer shorts…fuck me, his dick is curled like a snake, a sleeping anaconda…it must be huge. Responding to my touch, rock hard it flings itself out of his pants. I have never seen anything as big as that, it is huge, a skyscraper cock, I'm not sure I want to go anywhere near that bastard. There's no way I'll stretch to fit it, I suppose lube might work or maybe I just need a fanny the size of a bucket. I tentatively stroke it and James groans softly with pleasure, I decide to try and give him a wank, although it might be a two hand job. As my hand moves rhythmically along his shaft, he kisses me…is my fanny tingling definitely not, it took one look at his monster knob and shut up shop. His breathing increases as he gets more excited, I can feel his cock start to pulsate…he's going to come any second. I don't know why but just at crucial moment I let go, he starts to come and his penis is flailing around like an out of control fire hose, it's swinging from side to side, slapping against his thighs. I'm having to duck as he sprays spunk all over the room, I dive behind the sofa…this is not erotic, not one little bit. Finally he finishes, he slumps on the settee with a satisfied look on his face, I knew there was something about him…mystery solved.

I emerge from behind the settee and just as I am about to

tell him I have to leave because my dog is missing me, we hear a key being turned in the front door…

'Shit, fuck, bollocks…my wife is home, she was supposed to be staying at her Mum's tonight, sorry Ann, you need to go right now!'

His wife is home, the wife he's just divorced for shagging his brother. My mouth hits the floor and I'm gasping for breath as I think of something to say…I don't know what the fuck to say. I grab my bag as he unceremoniously pushes me out of the back door into the garden…'Sorry Ann, I'll be in touch.' I'm in a state of shock as I negotiate the herbaceous border and try not to knock over any plant pots. I try to quietly let myself out of the back gate, only I'm not quiet enough and the dog next door starts to bark. I see their lights go on and I feel like shouting 'sorry to disturb you, but I've just been wanking off James next door whilst his wife was visiting her Mother' My head is spinning, not only does he have a gargantuan cock, he still has a wife. Did she have an affair with his twin brother, does he even have a twin brother? He's clearly not been single for the last two years. What a fucking lying piece of shit, making me feel sorry for him so he could get near me with his donkey dick, no wonder he took so long to get back to me, no wonder he always walked ahead of me and no wonder he was always so formal in public…the cheeky cunt. His poor wife, I feel like marching back into the house and telling her exactly what her husband has been up to, but she'll have enough on her plate trying to clean up her newly pebble dashed sitting room.

I feel like giving up. I think I need to forget about Erotica, forget about men and forget about the fanny tingles. Date number four and I haven't had the sniff of a shag, I've had muff testicles, a burnt cock, scary Sylvia, a whipped arse and Godzilla dick…but no sex. I really don't know what I'm doing wrong, but you know what, I've changed my mind I'm not giving up because James is a devious, cheating wanker. I've clearly been unfortunate with my dates but my sexual Mr Right is out there somewhere. Onwards and upwards…please let me get some upwards!

It's late by the time I get home, I pour myself a gin and tonic nightcap as I reflect on the events of the last few hours, my phone pings and it's big dick;

'I'm really sorry about tonight, things are complicated but I'd really like to see you again.'

Too right they're complicated, you have a wife mate, he'd really like to see me again…he has no moral compass at all, he's obviously driven by his unfeasibly large cock and doesn't give a shit about his poor wife at home. I don't bother to respond I just block the cheating bastard, I'm not going to lose any sleep over that twat.

When I wake up it's a beautiful sunny day, the sort of day that makes you feel alive. I feel strangely positive, ok so It's not gone too well so far, but statistically speaking I've got to be due a success next. I haven't had any pings for days now, no dick pics (I'm strangely starting to miss them) and no messages from potential dates. I'm beginning to wonder if word has spread amongst the men on the site that I am to be avoided at all costs:

'Don't go near that one mate, she nearly burnt some poor sod's knob off'

'That Ann's a right slut, she flashed her tits at a little old lady'

'Fucking hell, avoid, avoid, avoid, if you slap her on the arse she'll break your nose'

'I wouldn't bother if I was you, she only goes for married men'

It really doesn't look good but none of it was really my fault apart from the lovely, lovely Daniel and even that was a freak accident. As if by magic my phone pings...it's a message. I open it and it's from Tom, he's the same age as me, a builder and very pleasant on the eye. I'm not going to rush into anything, I'm going to take it steady...we're meeting for a pizza tomorrow.

CHAPTER 6

Tom

    I'm meeting Tom in a few hours, am I excited…sort of. The postman has just come and the naughty bits I ordered a couple of weeks ago have arrived, the postman has obviously read the back of the package again as he gives me a wink as he hands it over…he's pushing it now. It's pink fluffy handcuffs and massage oil, if I'm going to be a paragon of Erotica, I need to be prepared. Handcuffs aside, I really have decided to lower my expectations, If I don't go into this thinking I'm going to have an amazing erotic experience I'm not going to be disappointed. But just in case I make sure my legs are shaved, my hair is straightened, my muff is trimmed and the handcuffs are in my bag. I dress casually, it is just a pizza after all. However, I have put on my red frilly knickers because you never know tonight might just be the night all my hard work pays off. I speak to a couple of the girls before I set off, they give me a motivational pep talk, though how useful 'don't forget to suck him off' is supposed to be I don't know. Erotica is much more subtle than a quick blow job…ok I know, I wasn't very subtle when I gave James a wank but what else was I supposed to do, that thing belonged in a zoo not my vagina!

I'm sitting in the pizza restaurant waiting for Tom to arrive, he's ten minutes late and I'm starting to think he's not coming. What the fuck do I do, I'm sitting here on my own like Annie no mates, should I order myself something or do I wait another ten minutes and then shuffle out hoping no one notices I've been stood up. Thankfully I don't have to go for either option as I can see Tom walking through the door. He's tall, tanned and muscular, he has floppy blonde hair and looks like he should be on the pages of a magazine not on a building site. Bless him, he's so busy looking for me he's just banged into a waiter on the way in. I stand up and wave (without the yoo hoo).

'Hi Ann, sorry I'm late. I couldn't find my wallet and couldn't message you to tell you I was delayed because I misplaced my phone'

I tell him not to worry because I had only just arrived myself, he was so apologetic I didn't want him to feel bad for keeping me waiting. We order our food and start to chat, I'm really warming to him. He's very down to earth, no airs and graces at all. He's actually a writer and until he starts to earn some money from his writing he's working on a building site. He's ticking all my boxes, tall, attractive and fiercely intelligent. The waiter brings our food and as he's making room for his plate Tom knocks his drink over…I think I need to add clumsy and scatter brained to the list. The waiter huffs and puffs as he does his best to mop up Tom's spilt drink and when he orders another I half expect the waiter to ask him if he wants it in a beaker. Tom apologises and explains that he's always been clumsy and he gets even worse when he's nervous...he's nervous, that means he either likes me or I scare the shit out of him. I tell him not to worry and resist the temptation to ask him if he wants me to cut his pizza up for him.

We chat like old friends, he did a degree in English and taught in a high school for a few years, but his real passion was for writing so he decided to take a break from teaching and is now writing his first novel. He hates working on the building site, he keeps dropping things and its not going down too well with his boss. I tell him how much I enjoy reading, although I don't go into detail about the subject matter, I don't want to scare him off. We finish our meal and decide to head to the pub.

As we are walking to the pub Tom gently takes hold of my hand...now this looks promising. I give his hand a squeeze and I look into his eyes, he smiles and we carry on walking. After a couple more drinks we are starting to get closer, he touches my leg, I touch his hand...I know, I know I've been here before, but this seems different somehow.

There's no awkwardness between us, no gaps in the conversation. I'm starting to think long term again. I remind myself again that I'm in this for the sex, nothing more nothing less, but he's so lovely. He looks into my eyes and asks the question my fanny has been aching for;

'Should we get a bottle of wine to take out and go back to mine?'

I'm immediately taken back to James who asked me exactly the same question, I'm tempted to say 'yes of course just as long as you don't have a monster dick or a wife', but instead I end up saying 'yes please'…too keen? It's a short walk from the pub back to Tom's house and we hold hands all the way back. Suddenly Daniel, Josh, Spencer and James become a distant memory, I think tonight's the night and my fanny is tingling just thinking about it.

We get to his and head to the sitting room, Tom opens the wine and brings me a glass. I've had a quick look around and there's no pictures of him with either his wife or his mother. We chat, but it's different, there's definitely sexual tension in the air, he wants me and I can't fucking wait to get my hands on him. He gently takes the glass out of my hand and kisses me, his tongue delicately skirts around my mouth, as he rubs my breast. I put my hand on his crotch and his dick is hard;

'Should we take this into the bedroom?'

Too fucking right we should, I nod in agreement and we stumble into his bedroom. He closes the door and I start to undress, not that I'm keen or anything but I'm stark bollock naked in five seconds flat. He attempts to pull his trousers off but ends up tripping over himself…but that just makes me want him even more. He throws me on the bed and starts kissing me but harder this time, he moves onto my neck and the gently sucks and licks my nipples, his hand traces my body as it moves downwards, he starts to play with my clit and I groan with pleasure. I start to move my hand up and down his shaft, his dick is big but not so huge I couldn't accommodate it, he starts kissing the rest of my body heading towards my muff and then I don't know what comes over me. I tell him to stop;

'Let's try this, Tom…'

I reach down and into my bag and get out the pink fluffy handcuffs, Tom looks like he is going to burst with excitement (I think he's even more of an Erotica virgin than I am). He slaps one of the handcuffs around my wrist and then attaches the other to the bed. He starts kissing and licking me again, tits, stomach, top of the minge…'fuck the cuffs are too tight, its cutting of my circulation!' Tom jumps off the bed to get the key and release me, he can't fucking find it;

'I'm sure I put it on the bedside table...'

It's really starting to hurt now and the more I move the tighter the cuff gets, Tom is on his hands and knees looking for the key…it's got to be somewhere. I'm starting to recall a horror film where a woman gets handcuffed to the bed and her husband dies before he can release her…'be careful Tom, you might hit your head on something.' He hasn't got a clue what I'm talking about and I'm sure he thinks I'm delirious. When my hand starts to swell and turn blue, in sheer panic Tom calls the fire brigade. He quickly gets dressed and covers me with a duvet, he can't apologise enough and I really can't be angry with him, it's my fault for buying shit handcuffs. You'd have thought I would have learnt my lesson after buying the cheap bell end burning candle. Tom holds my free hand and tries to be reassuring, it seems to be an age before we hear a knock at the door. Tom goes to answer it and returns followed by three firemen, cue some cheesy music and this would really start to look like a bad porn movie. I'm completely naked, handcuffed to a bed and surrounded by fit fire fighters. Just as it couldn't get any more embarrassing a fourth fireman enters the bedroom;

'Ann, is that you, what the fuck have you been up to?'

It's my fucking cousin Adrian, I knew he'd joined the fire brigade but I thought he was still training, well that's it, the whole family is going to know about this now. I can't even look at him, cheeky bastard, when we were little he'd always try and get one up on me…couldn't wait to blame me for all the shit he'd get up to. He kneels down beside me and is actually quite nice as explains that they are going to cut through the chain attaching the cuffs to the bed and then they'll try and get the cuff off my wrist. I decide not to look and Tom lies beside me and continues to hold my other hand as the firemen try and free me from yet another erotic disaster. It hardly takes them any time at all to get my hand out of the cuff. I am so grateful and keep thanking them over and over again, as they leave Adrian reminds me that it's Aunty Maureen's birthday next week and not to forget the party, everyone is going to be there (yeah, everyone except me) and not to worry he won't tell my Mum. He won't tell my Mum but he'll make sure everyone else in the family knows…oh the humiliation!

My hand hurts, my muff is empty and I'm dying with embarrassment, Tom is lovely, he lies down next to me and gives me a lovely cuddle, within a few minutes we both fall asleep. I wake up after a couple of hours with a throbbing pain in my wrist, shit my hand is swollen, fuck am I going to have to go to hospital…no fucking way, I just can't. I try and get back to sleep, but it's just too painful. I wake Tom up and ask if he has any painkillers. He's really concerned and insists on taking me to A&E, he thinks I might need an x-ray. I'm hoping it will be third time lucky and Little Miss Smug Bitch won't be working, it's not;

'So you've come to A&E today because your partner handcuffed you to the bed and you think you've broken your wrist?'

Well, he's not my partner, but I really wish he was and yes I know, I'm a walking erotic nightmare. Yet again I have to wait for hours before I get to see the doctor (I feel guilty wasting their time with my self-inflicted sex game injuries). Tom is so attentive, he brings me coffee and chocolate and keeps asking if I'm alright. When I eventually get seen it's just my luck that it's Dr Gorgeous again, he almost starts laughing as soon as he sees me…'Hello again' he says with a wry smile, 'What can I do for you today'…Oh come on, he's taking the piss now. He has a feel of my wrist and although it hurts the very thought of Dr Gorgeous touching me sets my fanny off (sorry Tom) he doesn't think its broken but just to be sure sends me for an x-ray. After more coffee and chocolate, Dr Gorgeous is pleased to tell me that my wrist is not broken but badly sprained, he'll ask the nurse to strap it up and I need to rest it for a few days, so that's my wanking claw out of action for a bit. Tom insists on taking me home, we share a taxi and as I get dropped off he kisses me and tells me he would love to see me again, I tell him to message me and we'll sort something out.

So, here I am again - no sex, not a shag to be had. I got so close this time, he was within sucking distance of my clitoris and I told him to stop, why the fuck did I get those bastarding handcuffs out…I must remember to complain in the morning, I think they need to send me my £4.99 back. I get into bed and think about Tom, I really, really like him, but have I fucked it up again. I've added faulty, wrist wrecking handcuffs to my roll call of erotic disasters, maybe I just have to accept defeat. I think I could live with shit sex if it was with Tom, I drift off to sleep and wonder what tomorrow will bring.

It brings fuck all! Its been two days and I've heard nothing from Tom, I think I'm going to have to accept I scared him off. My phone pings and I hope it's him, I look at it and fuck me it's a guy in a red morph suit, he's on his hands and knees, and he appears to have what looks like a marrow shoved up his arse…what the fuck does he want me to say to that:

'Nice morph suit but I don't think red is your colour!'

'Is that a marrow shoved up your arse or are you just pleased to see me?'

I delete the message and decide to delete my profile at the

same time, I'm done with this shit. Just as I decide to take a complete break from dating and put my erotic adventure on ice there's a knock on the door. I'm not expecting anyone and I haven't ordered anything recently. I open it and to my surprise it's a vision in blue jeans…Tom;

'Hi Ann, I'm so sorry I dropped my phone when I got home the other night, it's completely fucked and I didn't want you to think I'd forgotten about you.'

I don't now what to say, I'm more concerned about the fact I'm standing there in my pyjamas and fluffy slippers, bereft of make-up and my hair has gone full on pube head. I lie through me teeth and tell him I didn't think he'd forgotten about me at all, I just thought he'd been busy with his writing. He comes in and we have a coffee, he seems completely oblivious to the fact I look a mess. He's still apologising for the other night, he explains that when he got home he finds the key to the handcuffs underneath the pillow I was lying on…why didn't we think to look there? He really enjoyed our night together and would love to do it again, but maybe without the handcuffs. Fuck me, I'm well in aren't I?…I've got a tingling fanny, a lascivious lady garden and I'd take him right here, right now if it wasn't for the fact I hadn't brushed my teeth and smelt like a camel. We chat for a bit then he has to leave to carry on his writing, apparently he's at a crucial point in his story, but to be honest I'm not really listening I'm fantasising about what he's going to do to me next time we meet. He heads off and we arrange to meet in a couple of days, he's going to cook me a meal, which does make me a little nervous after last time...can you imagine 'Hi Ann, meet my Mum, she's come to visit for a few days.' I'm sure it will be fine, I can't be that fucking unlucky, can I?

CHAPTER SEVEN

Tom Again

I've been ridiculously happy for the past couple of days, Tom managed to get his phone fixed and we've been messaging and chatting regularly. He's a genuinely nice guy, he's intelligent, he doesn't have a clue how good looking he is, he's interested in what I have to say and although he has a tendency to walk into doors, his clumsiness adds to his charm. I can't tell you how much I'm looking forward to tonight. I've taken the day off work so I can spend the whole day getting ready, I want tonight to be perfect. As I always do before a date I've re-read some of my Erotica, thankfully my wrist has returned to normal so I won't have to try an awkward left hand wank. According to my books, I really need to aim for him fucking me over the work top in the kitchen, that seems quite popular and if he can do it over the sink that's a bonus. I think I'll give BDSM a miss for now since that didn't work out too well last time and I'm not sure about him penetrating both holes at the same time, that comes across as a bit greedy to me and it's making my head spin thinking just how he'd do it. I certainly still have a lot to learn, but maybe Tom and I can go on an erotic adventure together…I know I'm getting ahead of myself, again.

Whatever happened to a good hard shag and a cup of coffee, no strings attached. Maybe I really want lots of hot erotic sex in a committed relationship…with Tom (yes, I know I said that about Daniel and Josh and Spencer, but definitely not James). Fuck I'm confusing myself.

It's taken me a while but I'm done. I've had the obligatory soak in the bath, my muff is trimmed and my pube head straightened. I decide my regular lingerie just won't do, so I ordered a peek a boo bra and matching crotchless knickers, you're in for a treat tonight Tom! I'm wearing a figure hugging red dress which shows off my curves to perfection and I'm wearing matching red lipstick so if he doesn't want me after all this I may as well give up. I might be being overly optimistic but I've packed an overnight bag, I've checked my packet of condoms and they are still within their use by date (just) and I remembered to put the massage oil I bought with the disaster cuffs in, you never know, he might want to lather me up before he fucks me. I do one last check in the mirror and then I message Tom to let him know I'm on my way and head out.

Tom is waiting at the door when I arrive…fucking hell he's keen! He looks at me and smiles, his smile alone is enough to make me want to drop my big knickers. He's obviously been busy as I can smell food cooking when I enter his house, I have a quick look around to check there's just two places set at the table and no mad mother lurking anywhere and I'm pleased to report it was definitely just me and him. Tom tells me I look stunning and gets me a glass of wine, the only thing I fancy eating at this point is his cock. I take a seat at the dinner table, he's cooked a pasta dish, I have no idea what it is but it looks and smells delicious. As we eat, the wine is flowing and we can't take our eyes off each other. Tom asks me if I have been on any other dates through the dating site…what do I say?

'Yes, I've been on a few and every one ended up a disaster!'

'There've only been one or two that have ended up needing hospital treatment...'

'I've not had many dates but I've seen enough dicks to last me a lifetime and let's not even talk about the guy in the morph suit...'

I decide to lie through my teeth and tell him he was the first and the last as I had cancelled my membership (you can't improve on perfection after all). Tom talks about seeing my profile for the first time, there was something about me that made him feel he needed to meet me and he was so excited when I agreed to see him. I really can't believe my luck, is he really saying all these things to me,

Ann without the 'e', dating failure extraordinaire. After we've eaten our main course he brings out pudding and when he pops a piece of chocolate cake into my mouth I feel like my fanny is about to explode. The food was amazing and I'm impressed that Tom managed to get through the entire meal without spilling or dropping anything. I offer to wash up…not very glamorous but it's a woman thing. He won't let me lift a finger, the washing up can wait, he'll do it in the morning. So let me get this right, not only is he fit, funny and bright…he's fucking domesticated! I'm waiting for the punchline here, is someone taking this piss. I've literally found the perfect man, surely there's got to be something wrong with him…or maybe, just maybe there isn't.

Tom clears the table, puts on some music and opens another bottle of wine. We head for the settee. I take off my shoes and curl up next to him, he puts his arm around my shoulder and I tremble with excitement. We talk for a bit, but the conversation is a little bit stilted, we both know what's coming and we both know what we want. He leans across and kisses me gently on the lips, not a full on snog just a lovely, tender kiss. He stands up and takes my hand. I try not to think about what happened the last time he took me to his bedroom, maybe I should suggest we pop into the kitchen on the way, as I explained earlier, Erotica dictates that I should be sucked and fucked on a kitchen work surface at some point. I decide against it, bearing in mind the washing up hasn't been done, I don't fancy getting pasta plastered all over my arse.

When we get into the bedroom Tom kisses me, it's a hard, rough kiss with his tongue darting in and out of my mouth. We start to undress each other, I slip out of my dress and he licks his lips when he sees my underwear, he traces my nipples with his fingers and then unclips my bra, my breast fall out and I whip off my knickers (I'm trying to maintain my cool and sophisticated exterior without much success) although with them being crotchless I think the idea is I keep them on. I pull his t-shirt off over his head and then help him remove his jeans and pants, his magnificent cock is standing to attention. He kisses my breasts as I gently run my hand up and down his shaft. We fall onto the bed and he's still kissing my tits, but then he start to move down, he's kissing my stomach whilst his fingers gently play with my clit, I play with his hair and gently push his head down, he's kissing my stomach, he's past my belly button now kissing me gently as he inserts a finger inside me and then I feel his beautiful hot breath on my pussy, he licks my clit and gently sucks on it whilst thrusting his fingers inside me…I can't fucking believe this is actually happening (for someone so clumsy he has amazing rhythm). I gesture to him to stop and he lies back on the bed, we get into the sixty nine position (all those hours spent reading are really starting to pay off now) and I trace his dick with my tongue, as I start to lick the tip I can feel him tense up with pleasure, I cup his balls in my hands as I start to suck. He parts my lips and explores me with his tongue again, licking, sucking and thrusting it inside me until my fanny is about to explode and just as I'm about to come, he stops…fucking tease! He lies on top of me and starts to kiss me again, my nipples are erect with desire, I pull him closer towards me my nails digging into his back, I open my legs and wrap them around his waist, I'm ready to let him fuck me, his rock hard dick is touching my lips and then just as it's about to finally happen I have an idea. 'Wait Tom, why don't we try this?' I hand him the massage oil and he looks fucking delighted. He flips me over and I feel the cold oil on my skin and his hard cock against my back. He starts to massage me, he begins with my shoulders and slowly moves downwards, before I know it he is massaging my buttocks (fuck, I know I'm paranoid about it but I hope he's not looking at my cellulite), he's kneading them harder and harder, I want him to fuck me from behind so I move onto my hands and knees and then when he's used all the oil his hand moves between my legs and he's rubbing my undercarriage, well this is new, I've never had a fanny massage before. He stops and puts his hands on my waist, I feel him moving his groin towards me, he's about to penetrate me… here we go, its finally going to happen! God, this is hot…no its actually really fucking hot, burning even. Me and my stupid fucking ideas, he was within millimetres of entering me, I was seconds away from a damn good shag and I have to get out the massage oil….I am such a fucking idiot! I jump off the bed and poor Tom looks so confused;

'Fuck, shit, bollocks, I think I'm allergic to the massage oil, there must have been some left on your hand!'

He looks even more confused as I ask him to get me some frozen peas. He runs to the kitchen and brings me a packet of frozen chicken fillets wrapped in a tea towel (he needed to do a shop). As I lie on the bed with a packet of frozen chicken between my legs I can feel my lips starting to expand, I tentatively have a look 'Shit Tom, I've got muff balls'. He hasn't got a clue what I'm talking about and takes a look 'Jesus Ann, you've got bigger bollocks than me, I think you need to see a doctor?' Do I fuck need to see a doctor, there is no way I am stepping foot anywhere near A&E, I can't face Little Miss Smug Bitch and Dr Gorgeous again. I ask him if he has any antihistamines and he goes off to check. I think I'm cursed, why does this keep happening to me? I was so close to getting a shag and now I've got fucking testicles…Johnny Big Bollocks rides again.

Thankfully, Tom has managed to find some antihistamines in the back of his cupboard, I take a couple and hope for the best. He is so sweet, he brings me one of his t-shirts to wear and lies with me as we wait for my angry beaver to calm down. He's being really assertive and is insisting that if the swelling doesn't go down soon he is going to take me to the hospital, you should never be complacent about an allergic reaction…I add sensible to my list of things I love about Tom. He strokes my hair as he lies next to me, I bet he wasn't expecting this when I had my mouth around his cock. I'm pleased to say that the combination of the frozen chicken fillets and antihistamine tablets seem to do the trick and after a short time the swelling starts to go down. Tom insists I stay with him tonight so that he can look after me…I'm not going to argue. As I lie in his arms, my fanny throbbing (not with lust unfortunately) I wonder if I am ever going to have sex, I'm getting a little bit closer each time, but its just not happening. I wonder if the universe is trying to tell me something, someone up there is definitely having a laugh at my expense.

I wake up in the morning nestled in Tom's protective

arms. He stayed awake watching me most of the night just in case…that's either really creepy or really lovely. I decide to go with really lovely. When he sees that I am awake, he tenderly kisses me on the lips, asks me if I slept well and goes to make me a cup of coffee. He takes ages and just when I'm thinking he's probably left his own house to avoid me, he comes back with a steaming hot pot of coffee and bacon butties…how did I get so lucky? I'm quite enjoying this, tucked up in bed with a gorgeous bloke drinking freshly ground coffee and eating bacon sandwiches, it's blissful. So where do we go from here? Tom asks if I would like to see him again, of course I fucking would! I don't want to leave, I'm getting my feet firmly under his table. We decide to give it a go…I am officially in a relationship, we're going to take it slowly, maybe give the whole sex thing a miss for a bit, which is fine by me as it means I can do plenty more revision. Tom is my Mr Romantic and my Mr Uninhibited rolled into one, he's wonderfully charming and horny as fuck.

CHAPTER EIGHT

Lessons learnt

I've been seeing Tom for two weeks now, we've eaten out, been to the cinema, gone on romantic walks in the countryside but we haven't had sex. After the last two near misses, we've decided to get to know each other a bit better. It's been a lovely romantic interlude and it appears we've gone all Victorian. Don't get me wrong I'm not going to be a born again virgin forever. We are both gagging for it and I'm sure it won't be long before he fucks me in the sitting room, kitchen, bedroom and bathroom, I want him in every room of the house and I want him to take me in every position imaginable. I want to suck his cock and caress his balls, I want him to lick and suck my clit until I can't take anymore. I want to sit on his dick and ride him until I come. I want to try new things and be the woman in every Erotica novel I have ever read. But until he's ready I'm going to have to make do with the dildo I finally remembered to order, when the postman delivered it, he was just about to give me another cheeky wink when I looked him straight in the eye and said 'it's a vibrator'. He didn't know where to look, that'll teach him for being a nosy bastard! I might not have a dog but at least now I have a rabbit.

So what have I learnt from the past few weeks in my quest for sexual enlightenment? Well I suppose the first thing I learnt was you really don't need a smooth, hairless fanny. My unfortunate hair remover allergy meant I had to let my muff grow and you know what, I've had no complaints. Let your fanny be, what's a bit of bush between friends. Free your minge, let it grow as nature intended and just do a bit of gardening from time to time. A good push up bra can make the most modest of tits look fantastic and big pants are your friend. They can still be lacy and sexy but they hide a multitude of sins. Suspenders and stockings don't really work in the real world (well they didn't for me), as you know I couldn't keep the fucking things from falling down and sacked them off. I wanted to be sexy, but for me it's more important to be comfortable, there was nothing to be gained from having to pull up my stockings every ten seconds and if they snag at an inopportune moment it could wreak havoc on your evening…see the next paragraph. I have to concede that stiletto heels are sexy, especially if you are stark bollock naked, but do yourself a favour, if you are not used to walking in heels practise as much as you can. There's nothing that says rank amateur more than going arse over tit on your heels.

I was so excited to see Daniel, did I tell you how fucking fantastic he was? Unfortunately, I learnt the hard that when you are preparing for your first erotic liaison, never, ever be tempted to buy a last minute candle from your local corner shop unless you can be guaranteed it conforms to British standards. I'm not trying to lecture you, but fuck me its better to be cautious than to incinerate your date's cock, there's nothing like second degree burns of the dick to ruin your evening. It's also not a good idea to consume copious amounts of champagne before you let yourself loose with said candle and I've explained about the stockings. Before I met Tom, I would dream of Daniel having a change of heart and unblocking me his social media, I longed for him to say he wanted to meet up again so we could pick up where we left off (minus the wax) the sexual chemistry between us was phenomenal but I blew it before I could blow him. Daniel is my one big regret, don't get me wrong I do really, really like Tom but I had a connection with Daniel that I just can't explain, I'd only spent a few hours with him, but it just felt right on every level. At the time he was everything I was looking for, I should have taken the guaranteed shag and lost the candle. I do have a little souvenir though, when Daniel's dick shrank the wax helmet that had encased his bellend popped off. I managed to put it into my bag without him noticing and now I have my very own wax mould of his knob, I shall treasure it forever.

I might be being a little bit judgemental here, but be wary of dating a 30 year old man who lives with his mother. Don't ignore the subtle and not so subtle hints that she is the most important person in his life. I thought it was strange that she made our picnic and cooked dinner, but was so desperate for a shag I didn't see the warning signs. I had a fucking lucky escape, it was a shame because Josh was lovely, but Sylvia was a monster. When you go into a man's bedroom full of lust and he has a full size picture of himself and his Mother on the wall, run as fast as you can because you are not going to be able to compete with that. I was lucky to get away before Sylvia went full on psycho. I still get messages from Josh, he wants to know how I'm doing and he knows I said I was taking time out from dating to spend more time with my dog but would I be interested in meeting up…he really hasn't got the hint has he? You need to ditch her Josh, how many women have you lost because they've been scared away by your bat shit crazy Mother. Your Mother, you know, the one who covered up my tits and called me a slut, the mad woman who stood listening at the door whilst we were about to have sex. I had a lucky escape there! Which brings me on to pets. Always have an excuse to leave on the tip of your tongue and an imaginary dog is a great way to get yourself out of tricky situations. We are a nation of animal lovers, so who would doubt you if you said your dog was sending you lonely vibes.

Do your research! Now as I've mentioned countless times before I've read a lot of Erotica (obviously not the right Erotica) but when Spencer mentioned BDSM I did genuinely think it was the name of a rock band, and I must admit when I saw someone wearing a BDSM t-shirt I did wonder what the whips and chains were all about. If I'd told Spencer that at the time he probably would have run a mile and I could have avoided the ensuing disaster and once I knew exactly what BDSM was I should have researched my subject better…maybe invested in some nipple clamps and a gimp mask? I really should have guessed what was coming from his dating profile…he enjoys horse riding, of course he's going to have a horse whip, I just didn't make the connection. It was still a shock and I didn't follow Erotica etiquette, I should have groaned in pleasure and pain, but I forgot and lamped the poor bastard. Not surprisingly I haven't heard anything from Spencer since that fateful night, in his eyes I was an absolute beginner and he was probably right. I do hope he's manged to find himself his very own dominatrix. Let's face it that wasn't going to me, I got ahead of myself and tried to play with the big boys when I still had so much to learn. Anyway, I was never going to rock the thigh high stiletto boots look, my thighs are too big and I wouldn't have been able to walk in the fucking things.

If you think your date has an air of mystery about them, tread with caution. Never let them draw you in to a sob story…James, what a lying, devious, manipulative fucking cunt. It took me a while to fancy him, but I was willing to mend his broken heart. 'My wife left me, she betrayed me in the worst way possible, I caught her shagging my twin brother'…utter bullshit! Always trust your instincts, when his unnaturally large dick announced itself, I thought that was his big secret. Christ it was big, it had a life of it's own and when it exploded it was a sight to behold…or hide from. He could make a fortune online with that fucker. Anyway, I digress, his massive cock aside, he was an arse and I didn't recognise the signs. Looking back on it, when we were out in public, he did everything he could not to be seen with me, walking ahead, choosing secluded spots and the biggest clue checking no one was looking before he let me into his house, which was full of photographs of him and his wife. I suppose it could have been worse, he could have told me he was in an unhappy marriage and rolled out the classic excuses;

'My wife doesn't understand me.'

'She's let herself go since she had the children.'

'We haven't had sex for ten years.'

Some men can be real shits. My best advice…don't let your fanny rule your head.

Finally, don't buy cheap handcuffs, if it looks to good to be true it usually is and if you are tempted make sure you know where the key is. Those fucking handcuffs caused me nothing but grief, and the embarrassment, I bet I'm still the talk of the fire station and then there's my cousin, I don't think I'll ever be able to face him again, he might not tell my Mum, but he's going to drop some pretty big hints. I know what he's like and he's never going to let me live this down, every family party from now on, he's going to make snide comments about fluffy pink handcuffs.

The massage oil was unfortunate and it seemed like a fantastic idea at the time, who knew I had such a sensitive pussy…it enjoys being stroked but mess around with it too much and it swells up like a puffer fish. I need to learn to let things flow naturally, I was so close to a shag and each time my desire to be an erotic goddess got the better of me, his dick was almost inside me and what do, I say…'stop Tom let's try this' what a fucking idiot. I just need to be me and what will happen will happen…however if Tom does want to buy me some Love Balls I won't say no.

So that's me, Ann without the 'e', failed erotic goddess,

dame of disaster, paragon of nearly but not quite having sex. My big fat erotic adventure hasn't gone quite as planned, but I've definitely learnt a few things, I've had my eyes opened to so many erotic possibilities and after all the disasters, I have managed to find Tom. As for the future, who knows. Will Tom be my Mr Right, will he join me on my erotic adventure. Only time will tell and I'm going to enjoy every minute of it.

Book 2

SHOES, THE BLUES & EROTIC TO-DO'S

CHAPTER ONE

All Good Things Come to an End

Reader...he fucking dumped me!

Everything was going so well with Tom, after our recent erotic disasters we had been taking things really slowly and I was more than happy with that. As far as I was concerned I never wanted to see another pair of pink fluffy handcuffs again as long as I lived. As I predicted my cousin Adrian, firefighter and professional wind up artist, did not let it lie - he spent the whole of our Aunty Maureen's birthday party making subtle comments about me being tied up and searching for the key to happiness. Thank God I don't have to see him again until Christmas when he'll no doubt bring the whole thing up again and I'll have to deal with my Mum constantly asking what he's talking about. Anyway, enough of my dickhead cousin let's get back to Tom. We had spent the last few weeks going on lovely traditional dates, we held hands, cuddled and shared tender kisses. He had showered me with roses, chocolates and sweet little love notes, I was blissfully happy and content. He was definitely my Mr Romance and the time had come to see if he was also going to be my Mr Uninhibited.

I was so excited and my fanny was tingling at the thought of what Tom was going to do me. I'd bought yet more lingerie and was sure I'd be completely and utterly irresistible, my muff had been trimmed to within an inch of its life and I was ready to go. I cooked us a lovely meal, well when I say I cooked I mean I'd reheated some M&S ready meals and thrown away the packaging! The scene was well and truly set, we hadn't taken our eyes off each other whilst we were eating and I'd even managed to lick chocolate desert off my lips seductively. I decided to take the initiative and told him to grab a bottle of wine and a corkscrew and meet me in the bedroom. I lay on the bed trying to assume my most erotic pose, he took so long I must have tried every position in the Kama Sutra. Confused and a little concerned as to what had happened I went back to the kitchen. Tom was standing by the drawers corkscrew in one hand and the wax mould of Daniel's bellend in the other. I froze on the spot, he'd looked in the wrong fucking drawer, why oh why did I not hide my little souvenir somewhere less obvious?

'I found this in the drawer Ann, it's obviously not mine it's far too big'

The poor man looked mortified and had probably just developed a penis complex. I just stood there gasping air like a goldfish out of water. What the fuck was I supposed to say?

'It's okay Tom, I prefer a more modest penis...'

'It's not what it looks like Tom, it's just a left over from a sixth form art project I did...'

'I like to collect bellends...'

None of those worked and the last one sounded a little bit sinister. I was completely at a loss as to what to say, but in the end Tom did all the talking, 'I'm sorry Ann, I thought we might have had a future together but I really can't compete with this, it's clearly not going to work between us and I think we should call it a day.'

With that he smashed Daniel's bellend down on the work surface and left slamming the door behind him. So my future with Tom had been shattered along with my souvenir of Daniel which had been well and truly squashed. As I scraped blue wax off the work surface I felt totally bereft, tears streamed down my cheeks as I realised Tom could have been the one, my Mr Romance and Mr Uninhibited. I'd well and truly blown it.

It's been two days since Tom dumped me and I've decided I need to move on, fuck romance that shit clearly doesn't work for me. I can't sit around moping and thinking about what could have been, I need to look to the future, set my own agenda. I'm a strong independent woman…I don't need flowers or chocolates (well maybe occasionally). I need to go back to my original plan, no strings attached sex, Ann without an 'e' erotic goddess and mistress of my own destiny! I decide to start as I mean to go on and try out the bouncing love balls I'd bought but been too scared to try. Who needs a man anyway? I take myself off into the bathroom and the balls are clinking as I take them out of the box. I don't bother reading the instructions as it looks self-explanatory to me. I'll just pop them in, go for a walk and see what happens. I'm all done! It was all a bit of a faff putting them in, but one quick shove and I was sorted. I have to admit it does feel a little strange, I can feel them jiggling around as I move…I'm not sure, I feel like a fucking wind chime. I take myself off to the shop clinking and clanking as I go, every time someone looks at me I wonder if they know, they couldn't surely? I'm still waiting for my fanny to start tingling, but I think I'm far too self-conscious at the moment. I'm sure the bloke I just walked past just gave me a knowing smile, maybe he can hear them? I take myself off home and decide to eat lots of chocolate and read some erotica…maybe that will do the trick.

So the chocolate and good smutty book have had no effect on me at all, I can feel a bit of weight up there but not much else, I try jumping up and down, hopping up the stairs and sitting on the washing machine during the spin cycle and…nothing! I think my poor foof is pining for what could have been with Tom. So that's that then, I think I'll just take them out and try them again when my vag is in a better place. I go into the bathroom to start operation love balls and realise I have no way to actually get them out, I have a rummage around and can't get to them, if anything I think I am pushing them further up. This can't be right, there must be a way to get them out. I'm trying to keep calm as I rummage through the bin to find the instructions, my stomach churns as I read them and realise that in my rush to pop them in I've also inserted the string which I needed to get them out! Fuckity, fuck, fuck, fuck with more fucks on top! Maybe if I stay standing up for a while gravity will bring them down. After pacing around for an hour and having another good rummage I ring around my friends, they all react the same way - hysterical laughter and then the suggestion that I go to A&E. I can't see I have any other options, fucking hell have I not suffered enough the past few days without having to endure yet another humiliation?

I arrive at A&E and head down, walk slowly to the reception desk. It's fairly quiet and I'm sure everyone can hear me clinking with every step. I imagine them singing 'shame, shame, shame, shame on you' as I walk past them.

Somebody just needs to ring a bell and the scene will be set! As I approach the desk my humiliation is complete as I see Little Miss Smug Bitch at reception, her eyes narrow as she sees me. She obviously recognises me, I've been here so many times I'm virtually family. I can't help but mumble as I try and explain what's happened…

'You'll have to speak up, I can't hear a word you are saying'

I explain again and her eyes narrow even more, her thin lips are twitching;

'You've come to A&E today because you inserted some…LOVE BALLS into your vagina and now you can't get them out'

Yes, yes and fucking yes! Why did she have to shout love balls? That was a touch sadistic in my opinion. My muff is clinking like a Newton's Cradle and my cheeks are burning with embarrassment as I sit down, safe in the knowledge that thanks to Little Miss Smug Bitch every fucker in the waiting room knows exactly why I am here. I find a seat as far away from anyone else as I can find and bury my head in a magazine.

It's not long before I'm called, the nurse shows me through to a cubicle. I explain yet again what I've done as she goes off to find a Doctor. Whilst I'm waiting it gives me time to think about my disastrous dating history over the past few months: Daniel, Josh, Spencer, James and Tom. Where did it all go wrong? Daniel, he was just perfect. Josh, could have been a prospect but for his psycho bitch troll from hell Mother. Spencer, gorgeous and charming but should really stick to horses. James, married fucking shit with a monster penis and Tom, lovely, kind, sweet Tom. I'm just about to start tearing up when the curtain swishes open and it's him...Dr Gorgeous a vision in scrubs. I immediately get lost in his beautiful blue eyes and welcoming smile, he walks towards me and I'm almost trembling with anticipation. I can tell you know, if my fanny wasn't chiming it would definitely be tingling.

'Good to see you again, Ann. Now what have you done this time?'

OMG, he said 'good to see you', I don't know what to do with myself, was it just a polite 'good to see you' or is he actually pleased to see me? He looks through my notes and asks me to explain again what has happened, I can see his in his face that he is yet again desperately trying not to laugh. I run through the whole sorry tale again, his eyes are twinkling as describe how I got the balls in with one large shove completely ignoring the fact that the string needed to remain on the outside.

'Obviously we are going to have to get them out for you.'

I'm horrified, I mean I really would love him to have a rummage around in my fanny, but not like this!

'I'm going to have a chat with someone from gynaecology and they'll sort you out, just remember to read the instructions next time!'

With that he gave me another one of his lovely smiles and disappeared behind the curtain. Finally, my fanny forgets that it's chiming like a carriage clock and starts to tingle. I think the balls are actually starting to work as it's quite an intense tingle…I can't have an orgasm in here, it just wouldn't be right! Thankfully just before the tingling reaches the point of no return the gynaecologist arrives. I take off my underwear and assume the position. She switches on the light and points it at my nether regions, oh my goodness my muff is lit up like Christmas tree…it even comes with it's own shiny baubles. I cringe as I see the speculum in her hand, but I needn't have worried it's all over in a flash. The Doctor hands me the still clinking balls which by now feel rather warm and repeats Dr Gorgeous' warning to always read the instructions before inserting a foreign body into my vagina. By this stage I vow that I will never be inserting anything anywhere ever again…but I have to add that doesn't include cock. I thank the doctor, get dressed and scurry past Little Miss Smug Bitch as I leave. I make a vow to myself that I am never ever coming back here, even if it means I won't see Dr Gorgeous again which would be a shame.

When I get home I immediately pour myself a glass of Prosecco and have a cigarette to calm my nerves…I know it's bad for me, but come on I think after today I deserve one. Although I am still sad about Tom, I can't let it hold me back. I have a life to live and I'm not going to be defeated in my quest for sexual liberation. I've decided to give online dating another go and I've reinstated my profile. I just have to remember I'm not in this to get involved, look where it's got me when I've let my feelings get the better of me? I can be an erotic goddess, I really can, I just have to be a bit more careful and maybe not so clumsy! I'm not going to be a slave to my phone and switch off the notifications before I go to bed, if anyone is interested I'm sure they can wait until morning.

The first thing I do when I wake up is check my phone, there are three dick pics but that doesn't surprise me now…I'm hardened to them! But I do still wonder why men feel the need to send you a picture of their penis, let's face it they are fucking ugly things at the best of times so what do they think is going to happen when they send somebody they don't know a picture of their schlong? Seriously, do they think I'm going to swoon and drop my knickers at the sight of their cock? Dick pics aside, I have actually received a message…Stanley, he doesn't say how old he is, but he's sent a fabulous black and white picture of himself, he is very handsome and he has a bygone era look to him, how very enigmatic. He lists his hobbies as playing bowls, dancing and fishing…he sounds traditional and a little old fashioned, he could be just the tonic I need. He doesn't mention what he does for a living, which is a little strange. Maybe he has a boring job and doesn't want to put me off.

I've been exchanging messages with Stanley and he's so sweet and formal, I get the feeling he's a real gentleman and I'm pretty sure he would never have sent a dick pic. So I've decided to meet him, nothing ventured, nothing gained and all that. I'd say he has the potential to be my Mr Romance, but my Mr Uninhibited?...hmm...I can't wait to find out!

CHAPTER TWO

Stanley

I'm seeing Stanley tonight, he wants to meet in the car park of the Red Lion pub. The Red Lion is one of the quieter pubs in the area and it tends to have an older clientele, but at least we'll be able to chat properly and get to know each other better. I've decided to dress casually, jeans and a top which shows a decent amount of cleavage, I get the feeling Stanley is a proper gentleman who won't want to rush things. He can woo me as much as he wants as long as he realises that I'm after a shag, nothing more nothing less. Tom broke my heart and I'm not going to let that happen again. I'm in control now and the only feelings I care about are below the waist. I couldn't have a long term relationship with Stanley anyway, can you imagine?...Ann and Stan, we'd have the piss taken out of us everywhere we went.

I've just arrived at the pub and I'm waiting at the rear entrance in the car park. There's no sign of Stanley and he's already nearly ten minutes late. It's starting to rain and my freshly straightened hair isn't going to hold up much longer, if he's not here soon I'm going to be a walking frizz ball. Hang on, a car has just turned into the car park, fingers crossed it's him! It's parked up and my heart starts to beat faster with anticipation, he looked gorgeous on his picture and I can't wait to see the real thing. Shit, it's not him, it's a little old man shuffling towards me with a walking stick. Why is he heading my way...maybe he needs help with something? bless him. I'm always available to help a senior citizen.

'Hello Ann, you look beautiful this evening, just like your picture.'

What the fuck, how did he know my name?...then it hits me like a ten tonne truck, this is Stanley! His photograph was black and white because it was taken over forty years ago. Why didn't I guess? The formal language, his hobbies, I mean who under the age of 60 actually plays bowls? It all makes sense now, he didn't mention where he worked because he's retired! The devious fucker has stitched me up like a kipper, he's older than my Dad and my Dad has just turned seventy. I thought Stanley could be my Mr Uninhibited, I suddenly feel a bit sick. The things I imagined him doing to me, I feel like an OAP…Old Age Pervert! My brain starts to work overtime as I desperately try and think of a way out of this situation. Then I look at his little face and begin to feel guilty, he's probably on his own and lonely. Oh, fuck it! I decide to have a drink with him, bring a little happiness into his life.

'Good evening Stanley, you're looking very dapper tonight.'

He did look very smart, he was wearing a tweed jacket with a open necked shirt and corduroy trousers, just the sort of thing my Dad would wear. Stanley puts his arm through mine and we go into the pub. I look mortified and he looks like the cat that got the cream. I decide the best thing to do is grab a table and get Stanley sitting down as soon as possible as even with his walking stick he doesn't look too steady on his feet. I go to the bar and order a half pint of bitter for Stanley (he's definitely not a Stan) and a large gin and tonic for me, I get the feeling I'm going to need a few! I take the drinks back to the table and Stanley gives me an odd grin as he wipes his mouth after a sip of his bitter, I'd say it was a bit leery but he's probably just pleased to be out and about. I don't quite know what to talk about so I ask him about his family, he tells me was married to his soul mate Doreen for nearly fifty years. They had no children and when she died last year it meant he was all alone, he missed her so much he decided to try online dating just for a bit of company. I feel so sorry for him and touch his hand to offer some comfort…he does that odd grin again and I'm sure he's dribbling. It's slightly unnerving, but I'm not going to jump to any conclusions, maybe his false teeth are a bit loose.

As the evening wears on the conversation flows and I actually find Stanley quite entertaining. I'm enjoying listening to his tales of intrigue from the bowling club, who'd of thought Phyllis would have caught her Bob behind the bowling club toilets having his balls tickled by Norma the ticket lady? They sound outrageous and I accept Stanley's invitation to go to the bowling club and meet them all. There's obviously going to be no hot sex tonight but I think I might have found a new friend in Stanley and if I can help with his loneliness then everyone is a winner. As we are chatting away, I notice the pub doors swing open. Stanley notices it too and his eyes are popping out on stalks, the woman who has just walked in is absolutely stunning, ridiculously glamorous with the looks of a super model. I look at her in awe and wonder if her date for the evening is better than mine? I don't have to wait long to find out, he follows her striding purposely to the bar, his walk looks familiar and when he turns his head I realise to my absolute horror that it's Daniel!

Shit, shit, shit, what do I do? He can't see me, not like this, not with my geriatric date. Though why I'm even bothered I don't know, there's no way I can compete with Miss Fucking Perfection Personified. I put my head down and try and blend in with the wallpaper, but just as I'm trying to be inconspicuous Stanley squeezes my knee, I'm not expecting it and jump up knocking my drink over in the process. The noise of my glass hitting the table makes Daniel turn around and he's looking straight at me. He clearly recognises me as he winces and puts a hand protectively across his crotch. He nods and gives me a half smile, I nod back and resist the temptation to ask how his bellend is getting on. I look on green with fucking jealousy as he puts his arm around his date's waist, he could so easily have been mine! He should have been mine, I think I will regret lighting that scented candle for the rest of my life. In an attempt to escape Stanley's advances I go to the bar and get another drink, Daniel has disappeared and I can sense Stanley staring at me. His eyes are burning holes into my arse, this really doesn't feel right, surely he's too old for all this? I'll have one more drink and then get off home, I think I've done more than my bit for Age Concern today.

As I sit down Stanley knocks his glasses case on the floor, he's grinning again and I feel sure it wasn't an accident;

'Be a love Ann and pick my spectacles up for me, my back is feeling a bit stiff.'

As I bend over to pick the case up and can feel his eyes

burning into my cleavage. Now I'm really convinced he knocked the case on the floor on purpose;

'Nice tits!'

He didn't really just say 'nice tits', did he? Now where have I heard that before…fucking hell, it's him, the 'nice tits' guy who sent me the dick pic with the bulbous bellend! Well now I know, It wasn't just bulbous it was fucking mummified! I put the case on the table and Stanley is not only leering at me, he's salivating, he's gone red in the face and is clearly over excited. I'm partly annoyed and partly worried for him, surely this much excitement can't be good for a man of his age? I thought he was such a sweet old man, well he had me fooled the dirty bastard. I stand up and I'm just about to tell him I need to leave when he looks at me, clutches his chest and falls to the floor. This evening just gets better and better!

'Help somebody please, think he's having a heart attack.'

The bar staff rush over and someone calls an ambulance. I don't know what to do, so I pat his hand and say 'there, there', it's the best I can think of given the circumstances. Even in the midst of a heart attack Stanley can't help himself, I think he takes me patting his hand as a come on. He heaves himself up with the last ounce of strength he has and tries to nuzzle his head into my chest. Thankfully a member of the bar staff sees him lurch forward and thinking he is panicking puts a hand on his shoulder and gently moves him back. Another one of the bar staff tells me to keep talking to him, I don't know what to say, how the fuck have I got myself into this situation? Seriously I am fucking cursed, I think I must have upset the big man upstairs because my entire life is a disaster. Stanley is conscious when the paramedics arrive, they run a few tests and confirm that he is most likely having a heart attack. He's asking for someone to find Doreen as the paramedics help him into a wheelchair, he keeps saying her name over and over and I start to feel sorry for him again. He's all strapped in and as he's being taken to the ambulance one of the bar staff shouts;

'Don't worry Stanley, we'll call your wife and let her know what's happened.'

Well that's just the icing on the cake he's got a wife and I've been lied to yet again. Not only is he a dirty old man but a lying, cheating one as well! I truly fucking despair in men I really do. They think about nothing except their cocks, even the old bulbous ones. I sit back down at the table to finish my drink, it may have been a shit evening but I'm damned if I'm going to let a perfectly good gin and tonic go to waste. I run over the events of the evening and come to the conclusion that I should give up and become a crazy cat lady…no that won't work I'm allergic to cats. Maybe dogs then, that's decided. I'm going to fuck men off and fill my house full of dogs.

I take the last swig of my drink and I'm just about to leave when to my surprise and absolute fucking delight, I see Daniel walking towards me. He's definitely heading in my direction and he's on his own! I plump up my boobs and flick my hair back off my face, I'll show him what he's missing! Suddenly a house full of dogs seems like a shit idea.

'Hi Ann, I'm so sorry to see what happened to your Dad, is there anything I can do? Do you need a lift to the hospital?'

My brain starts to work overtime, he thinks Stanley is my Dad not my date and he's offering to take me to the hospital, just me and Daniel, alone in his car…I couldn't, could I?

'Thanks Daniel, that would be really kind of you.'

I fucking did, oh come on it's far too good an opportunity to miss! I get into Daniel's car, it smells of his aftershave and I'm getting muff tingles. We sit in silence as he sets off and can't help myself, I have to ask…

'I know I've said it before, but I'm so sorry about what happened last time we met…how is your bellend?'

Shit, maybe that was a bit blunt.

'It's ancient history Ann, best left in the past.'

What does that mean, has he forgiven me? Is his bellend okay? I resolve to not mention it again, I'm just going to enjoy the few minutes I have in his company. It does feel a little awkward as we chat politely about the weather, bearing in mind the last time I saw him I was stark bollock naked (apart from my defective stockings). I am wondering what happened to Miss Fucking Perfection Personified, but don't want to ruin the moment so I don't ask. She was probably his sister or the cleaning lady. We arrive at the hospital and Daniel has been nothing but polite and charming;

'Do you want me to come in with you, you might need some moral support?'

He is just perfect, but no I fucking don't want him to come in with me to see my imaginary Dad. I decline politely and quickly write down my mobile number;

'That's very kind of you Daniel, but the rest of the family are on their way so I'll be fine. Here's my number again, call me anytime to find out how Dad is getting on.'

I wave at him from the hospital entrance and as soon as I'm sure he's gone I jump into a taxi. I feel wicked and I'm sure I'm going to hell, but eternal damnation will be worth it if I get another chance with Daniel!

I'm home and feeling quite pleased with myself, I

managed to snatch victory from the jaws of defeat this evening. I've not only managed to spend time with Daniel again, he's now got my number. I look at my phone just in case Daniel has called already and I didn't hear the phone ring. No missed calls but someone has looked at my dating profile and left a message. What would this one be, serial adulterer, pensioner, spanking fan? Actually he looks quite nice, Andrew. He's thirty four, which is perfect. Works in marketing, so we'll have something to talk about and he enjoys long countryside walks…ooh he could be my Heathcliff. I go to bed and although I'm excited about Andrew I can't stop thinking about Daniel. Would he call me? Would I ever get the chance to redeem myself? I drift off to sleep and wonder what tomorrow would bring.

CHAPTER THREE

Andrew

Today I'm meeting Andrew, we're going for a walk in the countryside and for a spot of lunch in a country pub...how very civilised! I'm really looking forward to it, I've spoken to him over the phone and I can confirm he doesn't sound a day over thirty four. I've gone through my usual routine, long hot bath, exfoliation and muff trim and now the only thing I need to think about is what the hell do I wear? I haven't got walking boots, so will trainers do...where the fuck are my trainers? Are jeans okay and do I need a big coat? This countryside business is actually a lot more complicated than I thought. I think I've tried on everything sensible that I own. I even tried a head scarf, but I can safely say the Princess Anne look does nothing for me, maybe because I don't have that regal extra 'e'. I've settled on jeans, a light jumper and I found my trainers at the back of the wardrobe. Andrew is picking me up in a couple of minutes so I quickly check my make-up, spray my perfectly straightened hair again and pray it doesn't rain.

I'm in the car and can't help staring at Andrew. He is gorgeous, even better than his photos! He has the most stunning green eyes and the cheekiest smile I think I have ever seen. Is my fanny tingling?...it most certainly is! It's going well so far, he's chatty and very flirtatious. I think I could be in here. We arrive in a little village not far from where I live, it's very pretty and I can see myself living somewhere like this, maybe with Andrew and a couple of beautiful green eyed children. I mentally give myself a kick, I'm not in this for the romance, not at all not one little bit. We park up and Andrew takes a picnic basket out of the boot of the car. Warning bells start to go off, this looks a bit too fucking familiar. I remember what happened the last time I had a picnic with a gorgeous man and all I can see is Sylvia snarling at me. Surely I couldn't be that unlucky twice? I try and put Sylvia out of my mind, I'm sure Andrew has a perfectly nice, rational Mother who absolutely does not interfere in his love life.

We seem to have been walking for ages and everything looks rather green. There's not an awful lot to see apart from the occasional sheep and the wind is starting to get up. It's all a bit Wuthering Heights and I suddenly feel every inch the romantic heroine. I stride ahead of Andrew trying to look sexy as the wind blows through my hair. I turn and glance at him giving him my best come hither look and just at the moment when I look my most seductive my foot hits a rock and I stumble face first. I put my hands out to break my fall and my left hand hits something warm and moist, I look across and can see straight away… it's a steaming pile of cow shit! Does nobody clean up after cows in the countryside, have they not heard of 'Bag it and Bin it'? Fuck, shit, bollocks the cow pat look is not sexy, not one little bit. Concerned, Andrew drops the picnic basket and runs over.

'Ann, are you ok? That was quite a nasty tumble, what have you landed in…oh dear.'

Oh dear. I'm sitting here covered in still warm cow poo and that's the best he can come up with? He turns around and starts walking back, are you fucking kidding me? He's leaving me here, in the wilderness…what if I get eaten by goats?

Thankfully I misjudged him, he wasn't leaving me at all. He was just going back to get the picnic basket in which he had packed a packet of wipes…gorgeous and well organised! He's very sweet and gently wipes my hand down, once it's clean he offers me his hand and helps me back to my feet. Only my pride is hurt but I'm going to have to work hard to re-establish my sexy, erotic goddess persona. Right now I just look like a clumsy fucker who thinks cows should wear nappies. It's not long before we reach the top of the hill where we are going to have our picnic. Andrew opens the basket and throws a rug onto the grass, it's all starting to feel familiar again and I wait for him to tell me the picnic was made by his Mother;

'I hope you enjoy the food Ann, I got a local caterer to put it together for us, they're supposed to be really good.'

Now I am impressed, he actually paid a caterer to make our lunch, how posh is that? We chat as we eat and the food is spectacular, prawns, couscous, satay chicken…I wonder if I should ask him if I can take some home with me, there's more than enough. I quickly decide against this idea, nothing could be less erotic than me asking him if he could do me a doggy bag. The sun has finally come out, feeling full and contented I lie back and enjoy the gentle heat on my face. I'm feeling drowsy and just as I'm dropping off to sleep I feel Andrew nuzzling into my ear, I can feel his hot breath on my cheek and whiskers are tickling me (which is strange as I could have sworn he was clean shaven). Pleased as punch and fanny tingling I turn to respond. I open my eyes expecting to see Andrew's lovely full lips but to my horror the only thing I can see is a big shiny snout, I scream in shock and horror…a cow is licking my ear…a fucking cow! Andrew who had also fallen asleep wakes up, sees the cow and bursts into hysterical laughter;

'It's just a cow Ann, it won't hurt you.'

It won't hurt me? It was sucking on my earlobe...I nearly got intimate with a cow! The cow is completely unfazed and wanders off, probably to leave another cow pat for me to fall into. Do cows really just wander around doing their own thing, should they not be on leads or something? I really don't think the countryside is for me, how is this romantic? I can barely hide my relief when we pack up the picnic and head back to the car, we're going to pop into a pub in the village and right now I could really do with a drink.

Sitting in the pub, glass of cold Prosecco in hand I feel much more in control. Apart from when he's telling anyone who'll listen about the cow incident, Andrew is great company. He's quite into the whole countryside thing, he tells me he enjoys the freedom of the outdoors, how being somewhere remote make him feel anonymous and at one with nature. I didn't expect him to be quite so deep, it's an attractive quality and I'm starting to like him even more. He's also very tactile which is nice, he keeps putting his hand on my knee so it's looking pretty positive, there really is an attraction there and I'm excited to see how this evening is going to pan out. We carry on chatting about anything and everything and two glasses of Prosecco in I'm feeling very comfortable. I'm just about to go back to the bar when Andrew suggests we leave;

'How do fancy a drive Ann, I've got something I want to show you?'

Well that sounds a bit mysterious and I have no idea what it could be, it's getting dark so you can't exactly see much. I agree and within minutes we're driving again. We head out of the village and down a dark country lane, I'm starting to get an idea what he might be thinking about and I'm getting muff murmurs. He pulls off the lane into a secluded copse. Andrew turns off the car engine, undoes his seatbelt and kisses me. A long, lingering kiss which takes my breath away. This is it, I'm living my erotic dream. I have never had sex in a car before…I can't wait! He kisses me again and puts his hand underneath my jumper, he negotiates my bra and plays with nipple, my neck arches with excitement as he kisses it. He quickly moves on from my breasts and unbuttons my jeans. He slides his hands into my knickers and roughly plays with clit, I reach for his dick but strangely he pushes my hand away. He's kissing me harder now and just as he senses I'm about to come he abruptly stops;

'That was just the starter Ann, are you ready for the main course?'

Am I ready? Too fucking right I am! Andrew starts the car again and we drive a short distance through the copse. I can see headlights in the distance and wonder if someone else has had the same idea as us. Andrew stops just short of the cars in front of us, he gets out and opens my door (gorgeous, horny and a gentleman). As he helps me out of the car he hands me a mask, it's a cat mask and I'm feeling a bit confused;

'Put this on Ann, it makes it more exciting when they can't see your face.'

They? Erm, who the fuck are they? Surely he means 'when I can't see your face'. Andrew has now put on a fox mask, so we are a cat and a fox...what the hell is going on? It doesn't take me long to realise, as we approach the other parked cars I see what looks like an arse pumping in the moonlight...my heart sinks when I realise it doesn't just look like an arse pumping in the moonlight, it is an arse pumping in the moonlight! Fuck me, they're brave shagging in the boot of their car when anyone could see. But its not just one arse, I count at least three in the back of different cars as well as various arms and legs hanging out of car windows, there's a group just watching and everyone is wearing a mask. There's so much cock on display I feel like I'm in a chicken coop. It takes me a few seconds to register what's going on and then it hits me…He's taken me dogging! Is this erotic, would I be living my erotic dream if I joined in…No I fucking wouldn't and knowing my luck I'd end up on Channel Four.

'I'm sorry Andrew, you must have made a mistake. This really isn't for me. I mean you wouldn't want to watch someone else have sex with me would you?'

'Damn right I would Ann, come on give it a try, you'll love it!'

The cheeky fucking bastard, he's seduced me all day, put me in grave danger from wild cows and now he thinks I'm going to shag a random stranger whilst he gets off on watching me. No wonder he didn't want me to touch his cock, he was saving himself for the shagfest he thought I was going to join in with. Well he can fuck right off! I tear of my mask and chuck it at his feet;

'No, Andrew, I won't give it a fucking try! You can keep your mask, keep your cows and keep your random dicks. Enjoy the rest of your evening but I'm off home.'

With that I head out of the copse relieved that I've had a lucky escape…I bet Heathcliff wouldn't have taken me dogging. Then it hits me. I'm out in the middle of nowhere, it's dark and I can hear cows mooing in the distance…do cows come out at night? I calm myself down and decide the best course of action is to follow the road back down to the village. I still can't believe it, what planet was Andrew on...planet fuck a stranger? What made him think I'd be up for dogging, was it the incident with the cow? Do I just give out dogging vibes, maybe I look like I'm into swinging as well? I'm muttering to myself all they way back which takes my mind off the fact I'm on my own wandering down a unlit country lane. It takes me nearly an hour to get back, I head straight to the pub, drink a glass of Prosecco in one and call myself a taxi home.

I'm home and have never been so relieved to be back in my little house. I resolve to never go to the countryside again. It's been a very strange experience and I'm never going to be able to unsee some of the things I've witnessed tonight. If dogging is what floats your boat then that's fine by me, but to be put into that situation without any warning was a bit of a shocker. To his credit, Andrew messaged me to apologise, he'd read the situation wrong and thought I was up for a bit of fun...yes a bit of fun with him, just him not with his countryside dogging crew. I don't care if he's sorry, he can fuck right off. He most likely sent the message whilst shagging the flamingo. I block him and remove all traces of him from my phone. I'm getting ready for bed when my phone pings with a message. I have to check just on the off chance it's Daniel. I would have thought he would have messaged me by now, if only to see how my imaginary Dad was. Unfortunately it's not him, but it's not all bad news. It's from Ethan, he's seen my profile and is messaging to get to know me a bit better. He looks really sweet, he's twenty eight, a bit younger than me and a mature student. Maybe I'll give him a go, I've never had a toy boy before. Think of all the things I could teach him: How to burn a bellend. How to avoid cheating bastards. How to get stuck in Handcuffs and lose love balls. How to steer clear of cows and mask sex in the countryside…the list is becoming fucking endless! My luck has to change at some point…doesn't it?

CHAPTER FOUR

Ethan

I'm meeting Ethan today. He seems fun, really down to earth and straight forward which makes a refreshing change. I'm waiting for him in town, we're going to a roller disco! It's non stop glamour for me at the moment…a fucking roller disco, what was I thinking? I haven't put on a pair of roller boots since I was ten years old and even then I wasn't very good at roller skating. I lacked grace, co-ordination and pink laces, a fact the other girls didn't let me forget. Thankfully even at that age I thought 'bollocks to them' I might not have been able to pirouette in roller boots but I was a genius on my Game Boy. I always preferred the company of boys when I was growing up, they were less complicated then the girls. I relished climbing trees and making mud pies…then puberty kicked in and they dropped me like a hot brick, preferring to hang out with the cool girls who had breasts and actually wore bras. I was a late developer and wore a vest until I was 15…oh, the humiliation when we got changed for PE. Thankfully by the time I got to sixth form I'd developed a bit of shape and the fuckers who used to hang on Julie Rigby's every word because they'd heard she gave her last boyfriend a blow job, suddenly became interested. I had standards back then and would never have considered Julie Rigby's sloppy seconds…I didn't know where their fingers had been!

I can see Ethan approaching in the distance, he's a lot smaller than in his photograph. He's quite slight, with sharp mousey features and he looks like a typical student dressed in jeans, baggy t-shirt and Converse pumps, he definitely has that 'pint of Guinness and a quick shag' look to him and if that wasn't bad enough, I am going to look like a fucking giant standing next to him. It's going to be David and Goliath all over again. Shit, shit, shit…I think I need to find a way out of this, I look for an alley way to dart down but it's too late, he's seen me;

'Hey Ann, great to meet you!'

He kisses me on the cheek and gives me a flirtatious smile, it doesn't give me any muff tingles, but it is quite endearing. He's so enthusiastic, like an excitable little puppy. There isn't an instant attraction like with some of the others, but he's kind of cute in a geeky sort of way…maybe he has hidden depths? Taking things more slowly is a good thing for me at the moment, I tend to get so carried away and then hit with crushing disappointment.

Ethan bounces ahead of me bounding up the steps of the building two at a time. I don't know whether to follow him or put him on a lead. We head in and I can hear music booming out of the rink, classic 1980's tunes…maybe this is going to be fun after all. We put on our roller boots and Ethan helps me to my feet (bless him, pulling me up must have taken every ounce of strength he had). He's really confident in his boots, I am impressed! He very sweetly holds my hand, I don't think it's because he's interested, I think he can sense I'm going to go arse over tit at any moment. We start off slowly and very wobbly, he holds on to me until he can feel I'm becoming more confident then he lets go and speeds around the rink, he's skating forwards, then backwards, he does a few fancy twirls and I must say there is something quite attractive about it. Despite my initial reluctance, I'm actually enjoying myself. After a bit of practise, I manage to pick the pace up to a bit of Wham, sing along to Whitney and almost moonwalk to Michael Jackson…however this was less skill and more trying to maintain my balance when starting to fall backwards and now somehow we are holding hands again and skating around the rink together. It's actually quite romantic and I must say I've impressed myself, I haven't fallen over once…I can actually roller skate!

Ethan smiles and makes eye contact as we skate, my imagination starts to run away with me. I imagine us alone and naked on the rink, he stands on his tip toes and kisses me masterfully. Taking control, he picks me up in his arms and I wrap my legs around his waist as he fucks me whilst skating (I'm not sure if this is actually physically possible but it's a nice fantasy whilst it lasts). Just as my fanny starts to tingle, reality hits. There's no way he'd be able to pick me up, he'd be flat on his back as soon as he tried and not in a good way!

We finish skating and go for a coffee and cake. I'm really starting to warm to Ethan. He's not classically good looking but his warm, funny personality more than makes up for it. He's flirtatious and has a naughty glint in his eye. I'm starting to think I could be in the market for a pocket sized boyfriend. I feel a pang of disappointment when he says he has to go. I really don't want today to end and it seems it's not going to;

'Are you busy tonight Ann, I thought we could try out the new Chinese on the high street.'

Am I busy, let me think…nope! I try not to look too keen as I accept his invitation. He kisses me on the lips as he leaves and I resist the temptation to pat him on the head. We really got on well today and I can't wait to see him again. Although I've not got that long to get ready and I get the feeling I'm going to have to be at my erotic best!

I'm meeting Ethan in half an hour and I'm nowhere near ready! I've had a soak in the bath and I'm as usual I'm buffed and exfoliated to the point my skin is actually glowing. I don't know how I did it but got water in my ear and I just cannot get it to come out. I've turned my head to the side, patted my ear, held my nose a blown out of my mouth and it won't budge. I need to do my hair and get dressed so I'm going to have to hope it pops before I go otherwise I'm going to have to put up with muffled deep sea hearing all night. I've decided on purple lingerie tonight, I don't know why but Ethan seems like a purple kind of guy, he's a little bit different so I think purple will thrill him more than traditional red or black. I'm wearing a floaty, flowery dress which shows a little bit of cleavage and quite a lot of leg, it's the right balance of feminine and sexy as hell. I'll have to wear flat shoes as I'd tower over him in heels. There's not a lot I can do about my monster arse, but I get the feeling he'll thoroughly appreciate it. Just as I'm about to leave I get a message, it's from Stanley. He's out of hospital and recovering at home, he's wondering if we meet up again when he's better…erm no Stanley not only are you old enough to be my Father, you also have a wife. I really want to tell the philandering fucker to piss off, but bearing in mind he's just come out of hospital, I let him down gently and tell him that although I really enjoyed our evening out, I'm now in a relationship (hopefully).

We're in the restaurant, it's packed and my ear is driving me mad. I can barely hear anything above the noise in the restaurant and I keep having to lean right over to Ethan whenever he speaks…I suppose its not all bad news, he gets an eyeful of my tits each time and I can tell by the look on his face he can't wait to get his hands on them! We're onto our main course and he's getting really tactile, a stroke of the hand here, a touch of the leg there. We're chatting about our past partners (he seems to have had about as much luck as I have), when he leans over and starts to talk quietly, he looks around to make sure no one is listening which I find a little strange. I have to really concentrate on what he is saying as a party has just arrived in the restaurant, they have been seated at the table next to us and the noise levels are making it almost impossible for me to hear;

'You know what Ann? I'd love to bash your back doors in, how do you feel about a nice bit of rear entry?'

'   That's very sweet of you Ethan, but you don't need to worry. I locked my back door before I came out.' He looks confused and starts to blush.

'No, what I mean is, how do you feel about…you know…fudge packing?'

'I thought I told you, I work in marketing. Nothing to do with fudge at all. Although I did help on a marketing campaign for some once.' I'm sure I told him what I did for a living, he's obviously feeling so horny he's getting confused.

'What I mean is, have you ever travelled the Hershey Highway?' He's starting to look flushed and irritable now.

'Oh, no I much prefer Cadbury, you can't beat a bit of fruit and nut.' I have no idea what I'm saying to offend him but he looks ready to burst.

'Oh come on Ann, you must know what I mean…have you got your brown wings?' His face has turned so red he's less mouse more tomato.

'I'm sorry Ethan, I can't hear you…have I got wings? No, I ordered the pork balls.' He's shaking his head and I think he's tutting.

'I'll try one last time, how do you fancy a spot of uphill gardening?' I can't quite make out what he's saying, something about my garden I think, but he's saying it through gritted teeth.

'I love gardening', his face lifts 'but I don't get much chance as I've only got a patio.'

With that, Ethan stands up and shouts so loudly even I can hear him;

'For Fucks sake Ann, do you take it up the arse?'

My ear pops and I feel water trickle down my neck. Just as I can hear again, the restaurant momentarily falls silent until the party next to us start to piss themselves laughing. I don't know where to put myself and Ethan looks absolutely mortified, he mumbles an apology and looks so crushed I tell him not to worry. It could have happened to anyone. Yep, most people end up shouting about anal sex in the middle of a packed restaurant at least once in their life…what a disaster! We quickly finish the rest of our meal in silence. I don't know what to say and Ethan clearly just wants to leave.

We pay the bill and do the walk of shame through the packed restaurant, I'm convinced everyone is looking at me and sniggering and I'm sure I just saw one of my old primary school teachers shaking her head. I try and crack a couple of jokes about me being deaf and him thinking I was taking the piss but Ethan just cannot see the funny side and doesn't even wait to find out whether or not I would have let him bash my back doors in;

'It was great to have met you Ann, but I don't think you and me would work. You would make a great friend and I'll send you a friend request on Facebook but I don't think we'd be right together in a relationship.'

With that he jumped into a taxi and drove off into the night. Who the fuck does he think he is?…I'd make a great friend, but I'm not right for him in any other way. Well he can shove his friend request up his arse, I was doing him the favour the ungrateful twat.

Another monumental balls up and I've come home alone…again. I think I need to contact some of the major TV Channels, I've got a great idea for a new series…'Dating Disasters'. I've got so much material it could run for months! I decide not to get disheartened, I am Ann without the 'e', a sexy, independent woman and I will fulfil my erotic fantasies. It's quite clear to me, I just haven't met the right man yet and just as I'm wondering what exactly the right man is my phone rings. Oh my goodness…it's Daniel! I take a breath and compose myself before answering;

'Hola'

'Hola' now that's right up there with 'Yoo Hoo'. What the fuck, I was trying to stay composed, I should have purred a greeting in low sexy whisper. But no, I channelled my inner Benidorm and now the moment might be lost;

'Hi Ann, sorry I didn't call sooner. How's your Dad getting on?'

I'm so delighted to hear his lovely voice for a split second I forget I'd made up an imaginary Dad to hide the fact I'd gone on a date with a septuagenarian;

'My Dad's absolutely fine, why?' Shit!

'Erm, because the last time I saw you he'd just had a heart attack.' He sounds a little suspicious, so thinking on my feet I manage to pull it out of the bag;

'Sorry Daniel, I've blocked it out it was so traumatic. He's doing well, making a great recovery.'

He doesn't suspect a thing, I really am going to hell aren't I? The rest of the phone call was lovely, Daniel was so concerned for me and I played my part perfectly...so perfectly he asked me if I would like to go out for a meal. It took me all of about a second to agree! I am so excited, I've got a second chance with Daniel, my Mr Romance and Mr Uninhibited all rolled into one. It's going to be perfect and I am going to give him the time of his life...once fucked never forgotten, that's me. I just need to remember to hide all the candles!

CHAPTER FIVE

Daniel Part Two

I'm meeting the delectable Daniel tonight and I am beyond excited. We're meeting at the Petit Restaurant again (thank goodness I've got a sympathetic bank manager) and if I'm going to be mingling with a load of posh birds everything has to be perfect. I've already had my hair done and now I'm waiting to get my bikini line waxed. As you already know I have an allergy to hair removal cream and after developing muff balls I decided the best approach was to go au naturale. I've been trimming and trying to tame my unruly bush the best I can, but now I think I need to leave it to the experts. I get called into the consultation room and take a seat;

'Hi Ann, so what am I doing for you today?'

'   I don't want a Brazilian, I just want to go with the plainest option.' I can't remember what the wax I want is called, but I know it's definitely not a Brazilian…far to exotic.

'OK, so were going for a Hollywood then?'

I haven't got a clue what a Hollywood is, but if it's not a Brazilian it must be the one I'm thinking about. She asks me to take off my knickers and jump onto the bed…it's been a long time since anyone told me to do that! I do feel a little embarrassed but console myself in the fact that the poor woman is probably looking at fannies all day long, and once you've seen one, you've seen them all. She asks me to lift one of my legs to the side, and confusion immediately sets in. I've never had this done before and I'm sure she knows what she's doing. She reaches for the hot wax and before I know it my left fanny flap feels warm…no, this is wrong. I didn't want my flaps done…when I said plain, I meant plain as in just an ordinary wax, not plain as in take everything off and leave me bare. Before I can open my mouth she pops on the strip and….rip! I'm so shocked I scream at the top of my voice;

'Fucking hell fire, what the fuck was that!'

I think everyone in the beauty parlour must have heard as one of the other beauty therapists flies into the room and asks if everything is all right. I explain, that everything is fine. I've never had an intimate wax before and it was a bit of a shock. I didn't want to admit that I didn't have a fucking clue what I had consented to. Much as I didn't want to, I had to carry on. I couldn't meet Daniel with one bare flap, that would be ridiculous. I brace myself for the inevitable pain as the therapist continues my de-bushing and feel nothing but relief as she finishes and applies wonderful cooling body lotion to my now bare nether regions. I look down and my muff looks like a raw chicken, lets hope Daniel likes it enough to stuff it! As I leave the beauty parlour and start to walk home I feel strangely liberated…no hair, don't care! I've had a Hollywood, I'm now every inch an erotic goddess. I can finally cross something off my list of erotic ideals…I know I said let your muff be, but this feels great and you can't accuse me of abandoning my principles as it did happen by accident rather than design. When I get home, I can't resist having another look, it's a bit red but I'm sure that will calm down before I meet Daniel. I've got a bit of time to kill do I decide to read some erotica before I get ready…or should I call it some last minute revision.

I put on a final coat of red lipstick and even if I do say so myself, I look hot. I've opted for a classic little black dress with modest heels and no tights or stockings. I've been practising flicking my perfectly straightened hair out of my face coquettishly, I'm going to give Daniel the full performance tonight. I've got a sparkly new muff and I have every intention of using the new and unopened packet of condoms in my drawer. It's funny how things work out isn't it? If I hadn't of gone on the date with Stanley I wouldn't have bumped into Daniel and if Stanley hadn't of had a heart attack I wouldn't be here now waiting to go and meet my perfect mix of Mr Romance and Mr Uninhibited. I feel like the universe is smiling on me and my luck is finally changing.

Daniel is waiting for me when I arrive at the restaurant, he is as gorgeous as ever and my fanny is not just tingling but vibrating just at the sight of him;

'You look stunning Ann, it's so good to see you. I hope you don't mind, I bought you a little gift.'

Do I mind, not a bit! I open the black velvet box and it's a beautiful silver initial 'A' necklace. I think it's silver but it might even be white gold…I'll check when I get home, I can't really start looking for the hallmark whilst he watches can I? He takes it out of the box and I lift up my hair as he fastens it around my neck…this is so romantic, it's like something out of a film. Get in!!! He thinks I look stunning, he's pleased to see me and he's given me a necklace. I couldn't have asked for a better start to the evening. We enter the restaurant and are immediately greeted by Marcel the maitre d', he looks at me with a flicker of recognition…you better get used to me Marcel, I'm going to be a regular from now on. Daniel pulls out my chair and I sit down marvelling in his magnificence. He's incredibly attentive and still so concerned about my Dad. I play the part of the worried daughter to perfection (the Devil is taking notes) and he touches my hand gently, in his mind he's offering me comfort, in mine my fanny is calling out to him. He really is so fucking fit it's unbelievable, his expressive blue eyes, his smile…everything. He orders our food and I'm praying he orders the oysters again, not because I like them, they are fucking disgusting, but I want to watch him tease them with his tongue again and imagine it's me. The starter arrives and its smoked salmon mousse in puff pastry, damn I really wanted to watch him in action with the oysters! We chat about anything and everything and the champagne is flowing. There's one question I have to ask him;

'Daniel, when I saw you in the pub that night, who was that woman you were with?' Oh shit, have I just made myself look really needy, why can't I keep my fucking mouth shut!

'She was my date Ann, but she left early…she said I kept looking at you.'

I can hardly compose myself, he was staring at me not at Miss Fucking Perfection Personified. Staring at me, Ann without an 'e' she of the big arse and wobbly thighs. I can feel myself start to blush and I'm so excited I inhale the mouthful of salmon mousse I'd just started eating. I can feel it at the back of my nose and begin to cough and gasp, Daniel leaps up from his seat and starts to pat me hard on the back, my arms are flapping as I try to explain I'm not actually choking but he carries on until he's convinced I'm not going to die on him. He looks so worried and keeps asking me over and over again if I'm okay. Half the restaurant is watching and Marcel stands in front of the table with his arms outstretched so no one can see, this is just fucking typical but it could be worse, at least he's not talking about anal sex at the top of his voice. Panic over, Daniel sits back down and I take a huge gulp of champagne. Marcel is glaring at me, I'm clearly lowering the tone and I think I'm on my final warning!

We get to dessert with no more disasters and over coffee Daniel surprises me again;

'So, am I coming back to yours?'

I'm really struggling to maintain my composure and my mouth starts talking before my brain can censor what it's going to say;

'Too fucking right you are.' Do you think I'm coming across as too keen?

Daniel pays the bill…again and we jump into a taxi. We can't keep our hands off each other in the cab and I'm not sure how the driver managed to keep his eyes on the road. As we get out of the taxi Daniel picks me up in his arms and carries me to my front door, I scramble to get my keys out of my bag and we tumble into my hallway laughing…please somebody pinch me, is this really happening?

We are kissing as we walk down the hall, fuck the bedroom, I drag him into the kitchen (rule of erotica number 32, you always have to have a shag in the kitchen). He kisses me harder and with more urgency as he lifts me onto the work surface. Daniel pulls my dress down to expose my breasts and as he sucks on my nipples he slips his hands into my knickers and gently plays with me. I unzip his trousers and he is erect. As I run my hand up and down his shaft he groans as he slips his fingers inside me. By this point I am desperate for him, I whisper 'take me now Daniel' in his ear and he moves my knickers aside, I guide his cock towards me and just as he is about to go in…I wake up! What the fuck, you're telling me it was all just a dream? I quickly touch my neck, no necklace. Then I check my muff and it's got more bush than the Australian outback…it was just a beautiful, horny, unforgettable dream. I remember Daniel calling to check on my imaginary Dad, we weren't on the phone all that long but after speaking to him I felt so content I must have fallen asleep. I get up and go into the garden to have a cigarette, I need one after the dream action I've just had. I'm starting to think that Daniel is nothing more than an unobtainable dream, he called me because he's polite, caring and perfect not because he fancies me. I need to move on and put Daniel to the back of my mind, although I wouldn't say no to another dream like the one I've just had…it was fabulous!

In the spirit of moving on I check my phone to see if there's been any action from the dating site and yes, as well as two equally horrendous dick pics, a lovely lady has very kindly sent me a picture of her vagina…how on earth do I respond to that?

'Thanks so much for the picture of your vagina, I was going to have a kebab for tea but I don't think I'll bother now.'

'I'd love to chat but I'll have to labia and leave you.'

'Is it winking at me?'

I think the best option is to say nothing, I don't want to offend anyone because at this point in my quest for sexual liberation I really need to stay open minded. Just as I delete the pictures my phone pings with a message, I cross my fingers and pray it's an actual message not random genitalia. Thank fuck for that…it's from Ryan. He's forty years old, an art teacher who lists his hobbies as rugby, football and painting. I wonder if he paints football matches? He doesn't look forty on his picture, which rings some alarm bells after the whole Stanley experience so I decide to go back to bed and sleep on it before I decide what to do. As I drift off to sleep I wonder what would have happened if my dream was real. Would I be snuggled up with Daniel now, my head lying on his muscular chest content in post-coital bliss? Could it have been the start of something more? How many bridesmaids would I have? So many questions, to which I had to finally accept I would never get the answers.

CHAPTER SIX

Ryan

I decide to leave it a couple of days before I contacted Ryan. I just needed to take a bit of time to completely get Daniel out of my system and I'm pleased to say I'm ready to move on and see where Ryan takes me. I'm meeting him later on today, we're going to the cinema which should be fun. I told Ryan to choose a film, so I've no idea what we are going to see. I bet it will be something intelligent and arty given that he's an art teacher. I'm dressing casually (I seem to be doing a lot of that lately) and have settled for jeans, shirt and my beloved cherry red DM's. As I look back on my recent dates I'm starting to long for a pint of Guinness and a quick shag, at least I was getting some sex even if it was a little dull. Now I'm having to content myself with regular Ann Summers deliveries, my local rep loves me…I'm her best customer!

I'm meeting Ryan in a café next to the cinema, he thought it would be a good idea to have a coffee first as we wouldn't be able to chat whilst we were watching the film. My heart sinks when a frail old man enters the café…shit, have I been done over again? This one looks even older than

Stanley. Just as I'm about to sneak out through the fire escape, I see a tanned, muscular arm reach out to hold the door open so the old man can get through with his walking frame. There standing before me is an absolute Adonis! Ryan is tall and extremely muscular. He has a strong, square jawline that makes him look like a super hero, I'd love to see him in a cape…just a cape! He recognises me from my photograph and waves. I stand up to greet him and he gives me a firm handshake…a bit formal, but never mind. He gets himself a cup of coffee and takes a seat opposite me. The conversation is a bit stilted at first, he actually comes across as a little shy. So I decide to take control;

'I haven't been to the cinema for ages, what are we going to see?'

That seems to do the trick as he starts to talk enthusiastically about the film we are going to see;

'I booked tickets for Death Knocks Twice - part seven, It's a brilliant series. I've loved them all and I can't wait to see this one. It's the final one and supposed to be the most gruesome, have you seen any of them?'

Well, that couldn't be further removed from an art house film could it? I don't quite know what to say, I haven't seen any of the previous films and I'm not a horror fan…I hate the sight of blood. I decided to be completely honest and tell

Ryan I am a Death Knocks Twice virgin and ask him to give me a quick rundown of what the films are about…ten minutes later I wish I'd never asked. Basically Death has gone rogue and he's indiscriminately killing people, so if you are a twat and attract Death's attention he'll knock on your door twice and kill you when you answer. The franchise has been so successful they've stretched it to seven films, which in reality means this film is going to be shit. I try and look as enthusiastic as possible when if I'm honest, I'd rather watch paint dry. I won't even be able to sit and stare at Ryan because it will be fucking dark.

We take our seats in the cinema with a plentiful supply of popcorn, as the film starts Ryan pats me on the knee reassuringly I think he can tell I'm not 100% looking forward to it. It starts off innocently enough with the classic cheesy horror film teenage party. The party is in full swing with lots of alcohol and noise. One of the girls is being loud, obnoxious and a complete pain in the arse upsetting everyone with her mean girl persona…this doesn't bode well for her. She's sitting on her own now because she's pissed everyone off including her boyfriend, Brad, and no one wants to speak to her. Just as I predicted someone has just knocked on the door twice and arsey girl gets up to answer it…don't do it! She answers the door and is greeted by the sight of Death who looks menacing in his hooded black cloak, in his hand he is holding a large, shiny scythe. Arsey girl screams in horror and before she can close the door (and before I can cover my eyes) Death swings the scythe and…chops her head clean off. It hits the floor with thump, my stomach lurches and I jump out of my skin throwing a whole bucket of popcorn over the couple behind us. There's so much blood, I feel a bit nauseous and slightly light headed. I scramble out of my seat;

'Sorry Ryan, I need to pop out and get some fresh air.'

I try my best not to faint as I make my way outside, I knew this would happen. Why the fuck did I agree to go and see a horror film? As I take deep breaths of air, I hear footsteps behind me. I turn around and I'm thrilled to see it's Ryan. I had half expected him to stay in the cinema and finish the movie, but he is so lovely. He sits next to me and holds my hand…are those fanny tingles I can feel? He apologises profusely for choosing that film and refuses to go back in when I tell him it's fine if he wants to carry on watching;

'I just live around the corner Ann, do you want to go back to mine and I'll get you a brandy.'

I t takes me a split second to agree and part of me hopes he'll be a real super hero and carry me home. We'd be like

Lois Lane and Superman. Unfortunately I'm walking, but he carries on holding my hand. I could be onto something here and I need to get my erotic goddess head on, once my head stops swimming!

Ryan's flat is just as I imagined it would be, all arty and bohemian. I stare at the paintings and pencil drawings on the wall…they are all nudes and really quite beautiful;

'Did you do these Ryan, they are amazing.'

'Thanks Ann. Yes they are all mine, I love drawing the female form…would you like me to draw you?'

Would I what now? An absolutely stunning, charming, single man asking me if I want to get my kit off, what would you do? I take a large sip of brandy and excitedly agree. Ryan shows me to his bedroom and tells me to undress and put on his dressing gown. As I get undressed I start to have second thoughts, are my tits pert enough? Will he be able to see my cellulite? Is my bush too unruly?...actually that's not too much of a worry considering how bohemian his flat is, he probably likes his fannies circa 1970. There's no turning back now, in for a penny in for a pound and all that! I get undressed and feel relieved Ryan hasn't seen my passion killing big yellow knickers and grey sports bra. When I'm ready I come out and he's waiting, pencil and paper in hand. He looks very serious and incredibly focused, he doesn't flinch when I take off the dressing gown and lie back on the settee. I feel like Kate Winslet in Titanic and I can't resist quoting her famous line;

'I want you to draw me like one of your French girls.'

Ryan looks at me blankly, he doesn't have a clue what I'm talking about. I explain about the scene in the film, he hasn't seen it so the reference is lost on him…how has he not seen Titanic! I move on quickly and try and adopt my most erotic pose, you really couldn't get more erotic goddess than this;

'Are you alright Ann, do you have cramp? You look a little awkward there.'

He gets up and poses me on the settee, his touch send an electric tingle through my body, there is definitely an attraction there, for me anyway. Ryan is being the consummate professional and is not at all fazed by my nakedness. I'm not sure whether he fancies me or not, he's not giving anything away.

Time passes very slowly when you are stark bollock naked and lying perfectly still on a gorgeous man's settee. It's actually quite boring trying to look erotic and it's the best I can do to stop myself falling asleep, thankfully the fear of dropping off and dribbling keeps me awake. After what seems like an eternity, Ryan tells me my drawing is finished.

It's probably nowhere near finished, but I think me asking 'are you done yet?' every few minutes was getting on his nerves…I've been like an annoying child on a car journey and I think he's lost patience with me. I put the dressing gown back on and Ryan turns the paper around to show me…it is actually finished and it's beautiful and very flattering!

'I can't believe that's me!'

'Why not, you're a very beautiful woman Ann. Your lumps and bumps make you real.'

Lumps and fucking bumps, cheeky bastard! He did call me beautiful though so I'll let him off just this once. He tells me to go and get dressed and he'll get me another brandy. That's a bit disappointing, I was hoping he'd want to see a bit more of me naked! We sit fully clothed on the settee and Ryan tells me about his love of teaching, he really cares for his pupils and wants them all to achieve their potential…magnificent and dedicated! I nod knowingly when really I'm just concentrating oh his face, he looks so rugged but gentle at the same time. We chat for an age and just when I think he mustn't be interested in me, he pulls me towards him and kisses me. It's the most intense kiss I think I've ever had, he starts slowly, gently teasing my lips. Ryan holds me tighter as he kisses me harder, deeper and more intensely.

I'm just about to reach for his dick when he jumps up;

'Shit Ann, I'm supposed to teaching an art class in ten minutes.'

Fuck, fuck, fuckity fuck! Every fucking time I get close, something happens! He keeps saying sorry as he ushers me out of the front door;

'I've really enjoyed today Ann, I'm so sorry I've got this class. I'll call you.'

Hmm, my suspicions are aroused so I decide to hang about for a couple of minutes just in case his 'wife' comes home. I've been here before with James so I'm sorry if I come across as not very trusting. I wait around the corner and there's no sign of anyone else going into the flat. I quickly check my phone for local art classes and it's there, Art for Beginners with Ryan Jones. He was telling the truth…you can't blame me for wondering considering the experiences I've had recently. I'm just about to head back home when Ryan comes out. I quickly fling myself over a hedge but I'm a split second too late and he sees me;

'Ann, is that you? Are you ok?'

Mortified, I drag myself up from behind the hedge covered in mud and pulling leaves out of my hair;

'Oh I'm fine, I dropped my mobile and as I reached over to grab it I fell. I've always been a bit clumsy.' I finish the sentence off with a girly laugh, I'm not sure whether I sound flirtatious or completely bat shit crazy?

'Just so long as you are ok, got to dash. I'll call you'.

As I wave Ryan off I feel renewed sense of optimism. I'm trying not to get over excited and have to remind myself yet again that I'm in this for a good hard shag and nothing more. Emotions are there to be messed with so I'm leaving them out of the equation…although I do have to say Ryan and me would make beautiful babies.

CHAPTER SEVEN

Doreen

I arrive home and I'm still on cloud nine after my afternoon with Ryan when Doreen calls. I don't recognise the number at all and break my rule of not answering numbers I don't know just in case it's Ryan calling me from a different phone;

'Hello, is that Ann? I think you know my husband Stanley.'

I'm completely taken aback and have not got a clue what I'm supposed to say. I immediately feel horrendously guilty, the poor woman. She's quite calm and doesn't kick off but she would like to meet me for a chat. What do I do? Tell her to fuck off and put the phone down, it's not my fault her husband is deceitful old bastard, or do I agree to meet her for coffee? I can't swear at an old lady so agree to meet her for coffee. She's already in town and the shops shut soon so we're meeting in half an hour. I'm starting to feel a little worried. What does she want, is she going to hit me with her handbag? Thankfully my conscience is clear, I had no idea Stanley was married…I had no idea Stanley was a randy old goat. How the fuck do I get myself into these situations?

Doreen is already waiting for me when I arrive at the coffee shop. She doesn't look as old as Stanley, she's incredibly glamorous and has a youthful glow. I get myself a coffee and sit down;

'Thanks, so much for coming Ann, please don't worry I'm not angry at you. I just wanted to apologise for my wanker of a husband.'

I nearly spat my coffee out! She's clearly not happy with him and has no intention of chasing me down the street calling me a brazen hussy, relief sweeps over me as she tells me her story;

'I was very young when I met Stanley and, well, it was a bit of a whirlwind really. He was incredibly good looking and such a catch. I should have seen the warning signs, he was vain and flirtatious with other women when we went out...he described himself as having movie star looks and frequently told me how lucky I was to be with someone so good looking. Unfortunately I was blinded by love but it didn't take me too long to get the feeling he didn't think I was good enough for him. We quickly married and had two sons. It was when the boys were small I found out about his first affair and I don't mind saying it broke my heart, but my family loved him and persuaded me to give him another chance, it was just a mistake they said. I ignored the little voice in my head that was telling me to dump the bastard. Things were fine for a few years, but as I got older and my face became more lined he started looking for excitement elsewhere. It was always younger women, he was so arrogant. I think that's what he felt he deserved, a younger woman on his arm as a sign of his masculinity. I learnt to ignore his moods, his disappearances and his fury as he blamed me for his infidelity. I can't tell you the number of furious partners I've had to deal with when they've come knocking to find Stanley…the man is an immoral shit with no thought for anyone else except himself. All that matters to Stanley, is Stanley. Even now when he should be taking life easy, he's constantly on the internet chasing young women, I don't know what he thinks is going to happen…who would have sex with that?'

I laugh out loud at her final comment, she's such a lovely woman who doesn't deserve a minute of what Stanley has put her through. I apologise to her again and explain that when he contacted me on the dating site he used a picture of himself as a young man and I also told her that he had told me she was dead and they had no children. I felt awful telling her but she didn't bat an eyelid, she had heard it all before;

'The reason I've come to see you today Ann is firstly to apologise for my husband's behaviour. I bet your face was a picture when he arrived on your date! I'm guessing your shock was soon replaced with sympathy because you thought he was a sweet and frail old man who had nobody in the world, until he started leering over you, then you must have wondered what the hell was going on. Secondly I wanted to say to you, live your life Ann. Don't let anyone put you down, I should have left years ago but I felt keeping my family together was more important than how I felt. I sacrificed my own happiness when I didn't need to. My boys would have been fine without Stanley, it wasn't like he was a hands on father in the first place. I've been with Stanley so long I suppose I had a form of Stockholm syndrome, I knew he wasn't right and I deserved better. But love had been replaced by familiarity and I couldn't imagine what I would do without him. It took me forty years to finally realise my life would be so much better without him. Do what makes you happy Ann and never let any cunt piss on your bonfire, you're only here once and you need to make every minute count!'

 I feel nothing but admiration for Doreen, she's a wonderful woman and swears like a trooper…she's fabulous and clearly knows Stanley very well as I couldn't have described our date better myself. How many women had that man had? Doreen doesn't say but reading between the lines

I'm guessing his little black book was bulging at the seams. I almost pity Stanley for not realising what he had, wasting his life chasing something better when he could never find anyone better than the woman he had at home;

'So what are you going to do Doreen? Are you having to nurse Stanley back to health?'

'Fuck that darling, I've wasted too much time on that nasty piece of work. I'm seventy years old and finally I'm going to start living my best life. Yesterday, I emptied our joint bank account and tomorrow I'm off on a round the world cruise. I'm so excited, I haven't been abroad for years. I'm going to see the world, I'm going to savour every second and you never know I might meet my Mr Perfect, Lord knows I could do with a good seeing too, Stanley hasn't been able to get a hard on for years.'

With that, I spit my coffee out again, I hope I'm just like Doreen when I grow old. She's fun, sparkling and deserves the best. I hope she meets her Mr Perfect, better still if he's twenty years younger…fuck you Stanley your wife deserves so much better! I wonder what he'll think when he finds out she's going? I don't think he's going to be very happy losing control after all these years;

'So what do you think Stanley will say when you tell him you're going?'

'Ann, I couldn't give two flying shits what he thinks. He's got enough food to last him in the freezer and I've okayed it with his Doctor. Our next door neighbour is going to pop in to check on him every day which will be hilarious because he absolutely detests her. She's a big talker and he finds everything that comes out of her mouth irrelevant, so of course I had to tell her he might be lonely and in need of a good long chat. I've wasted forty years of my life on that man and I don't intend to waste another minute.'

She really is inspirational, I get up and give her a big hug, she's freed herself from her shackles and I have nothing but admiration for her. We chat for a bit longer before we finish our coffee and she promises to keep in touch. I do hope she does, I would love to know what happens on her cruise. We say our goodbyes and just as Doreen is leaving she turns back;

'Remember Ann, you only get one shot at life so be happy.'

I sit back and reflect on the conversation we've just had, Doreen is right in everything she's saying. As much as I admire her, I don't want to get to seventy and feel like I've wasted a moment of my life, I don't want to have any regrets or think 'what if'. So I really need to go for it with Ryan. I can succeed in my quest for sexual liberation, I can be an erotic goddess, but maybe a bit of romance as well wouldn't be a bad thing.

CHAPTER EIGHT

Ryan (again)

I just got back from my coffee with Doreen when Ryan called. I think he must be interested, he called me as soon as his art class finished. After a couple of days messaging and chatting over the phone we are meeting up tonight. He has VIP tickets for a new wine bar in town and I'm his plus one…check me out, I'm a VIP now. Finally I can actually get dressed up to the nines, I feel like I've been wearing nothing but jeans recently. I'm going for a long silver cocktail dress which is split up to the thigh and in the best tradition of erotic goddesses, I've bought myself a pair of six inch patent leather stilettos. As you may remember, I have tried and failed in high heeled shoes before and these fuckers are even higher so today, I am going to take my own advice and I am mainly going to be learning to walk in them. I get them out of the box and fuck, they are high! They slip on easily and actually feel quite comfortable, standing up is a challenge and I wobble slightly until I manage to get my balance. I do a few circuits of the house, go up and down the stairs a couple of times and you know what, I think I've got it! If my 'fuck me' shoes don't get me a shag tonight I think may as well give up!

I've spent the rest of the afternoon getting ready, I've done the obligatory muff trim, sorted out my unruly armpits and now I'm waiting for Ryan to arrive. I'm wearing my hair up for a change. I think an 'up do' suits a cocktail dress. Ha, listen to me, who the fuck do I think I am…stylist to the stars? I hear a car pull up outside and forget I'm wearing skyscraper heels as I rush out of the front door, I wobble and it feels like I'm going over but somehow, by some miracle I manage to regain my balance without anybody noticing (note to self…do not under any circumstances run in these shoes). I get into the taxi and Ryan looks edible in his black suit, think James Bond but better looking and more charming. He kisses me on the cheek and immediately takes hold of my hand, my fanny starts to tingle…something tells me she's going to get a damn good seeing to later on.

I feel like I'm at the Oscars, we step out of the taxi and walk down a red carpet to get in, the local press are taking photographs and I actually feel quite important. There's a waiter standing at the entrance handing out complimentary glasses of champagne…I don't mind if I do. The wine bar itself is festooned with balloons and twinkly lights…suddenly my imagination takes me to my wedding reception, Ryan sweeps me up in his arms as we are about to do the first dance...I just can't help myself can I? I'm brought back down to earth when Ryan asks if I'd like a glass or bottle of Prosecco? I've already got champagne and I need to keep my wits about me tonight so opt for just a glass. I find a table as he waits at the bar, I don't think I ever seen so many glamorous women in one place at the same time. I do find them slightly intimidating, I feel like I'm back in the changing rooms at school again, slightly inadequate and lacking in the chest department. The bar is awash with sequins and fake tits and the smell of fake tan hangs heavily in the air. Clearly on the prowl (bitches...) they start to encircle Ryan at the bar, they are hunting him down like a pack of hyenas. I watch him carefully, I'm intrigued as to what he's going to do. They are almost on top of him now trout pouting as if their lives depended on it, one woman is literally trying to thrust her more than ample bosom in his face. Ryan isn't fazed by them at all. To my absolute delight, he gently moves them out of the way, walks purposefully to our table and kisses me on the lips...take that slags!

Our table is right next to the dance floor and every opportunity I get, I slip my shoes off to let my poor feet recover. Ryan is such good company, I haven't laughed so much in ages. He keeps dragging me onto the dance floor which is a bit tricky as I have to put my shoes back on each time. He's a very good mover, we've danced quickly, we've danced slowly…I swear he thinks he's on Strictly Come Dancing! Every time we hit the dance floor I feel the hyenas watching, but Ryan only has eyes for me. I love that they can't understand why he isn't giving them a second glance….he's with me and he's happy, he clearly likes my natural breasts and my lumps and bumps (as he puts it) make me real. I've had a wonderful evening, we've laughed, danced and kissed all night long and he made a point of introducing me to his friends, which is a good sign isn't it? Neither of us want the night to end so we go back to his. When we arrive we head straight for the living room and Ryan pours us both a large brandy. I notice that the picture he drew of me has been framed and takes pride of place over the fire place. He sees me looking at it;

'It took everything I had to stay professional whilst I drew you, I wanted you so badly.'

Fucking hell, did he really just say what I thought he just said? Is this another dream? I surreptitiously pinch myself, it hurts…I'm not dreaming! He stands up and I walk towards him like the erotic goddess I know I can be. He takes me in my arms and kisses me, he expertly unzips my dress and it falls to the floor. Next he undoes my bra and flings it across the room. He picks up his glass of brandy, drips it across my breasts and licks it off as he plays with my nipples. His hand reaches into my knickers, he expertly parts my lips with his fingers and teases my clit. I'm wet and judging by what I've just felt in his trousers, he's ready to explode. I unzip him, drop to my knees and start to suck his cock, he groans and gently pulls my hair. Ryan tells me to stop, he wants to fuck me…finally I'm going to get a decent shag. He pulls off his trousers, I throw off my knickers and I'm just about to take off my shoes when he says;

'No Ann, keep the shoes on, they're sexy as hell!'

Whatever turns him on…I knew the shoes were a good idea! He's sitting on the settee his huge erection waiting for me. I step towards him, I'm completely naked apart from my shoes, I'm living my erotic dream! Look at me posh bird from 50 Shades of Grey, this is how you do it! I suck my stomach in and walk seductively towards him. His arms are outstretched, his cock is beckoning me and I'm just about there when my ankle goes…stupid fucking shoes! I feel myself falling, everything happens in slow motion, I hit my head on a side table and then nothing…until;

'Hello Ann, Ann, can you hear me my name is Mark I'm a paramedic.'

He's a para what now? I feel woozy and my head hurts;

'We're going to take you to hospital Ann, you've had

nasty bang to the head and I think we need to get a Doctor to take a look at you.'

Thankfully Ryan covered me with a throw before the paramedics arrived and now he retrieves my knickers from behind the settee and gives me one of his shirts to put on so I don't feel so exposed. He insists on coming to the hospital with me and holds my hand in the ambulance. I think this one is definitely a keeper.

'I'm so sorry Ryan, it was such a lovely evening and I've ruined it.' I feel like crying, until…

'You've ruined nothing, there'll be other evenings…if you want?'

If I want, are you joking of course I want. I squeeze his hand tighter and my fanny would be tingling if my head wasn't throbbing so much. We arrive at the hospital and the ambulance crew wheel me in. I can't believe my luck, Little Miss Smug Bitch isn't on reception and the lady who books me in is absolutely lovely. I'm taken through to a cubicle and I don't care how long I have to wait, Ryan is with me and I feel blissfully happy. A nurse pops her head around the curtain and tells me it won't be too long before a Doctor comes to see me. So that means it won't be long until I'm sandwiched between the lovely Ryan and Dr Gorgeous. The bump on my head although painful and unattractive may actually have been worth it!

I send Ryan off to get himself a coffee, it's been a long night and he's starting to look a bit tired. Within seconds of him leaving the nurse pops her head around the cubicle and tells me the Doctor is on their way. I brace myself for Dr Gorgeous and since it's just going to be me and him, I unbutton the shirt I'm wearing so I show a little cleavage and as I'm still wearing those stupid fucking shoes I decide to use them to my advantage. I throw off the sheet that's covering me and cross my legs seductively...I'm waiting Dr G. As the curtain to my cubicle is slowly being drawn back I feel butterflies in my stomach, I smile seductively until I see the Doctor. To my horror, it's not Dr Gorgeous it's...Sylvia, Josh's mother! Fuck, I had no idea she was a Doctor! How the hell is that woman a Doctor? She's got the bedside manner of a serial killer! She's just standing there starting at me, her piercing eyes narrow and flicker of recognition crosses her face. I see her staring at my shoes and I'm sure she mouths 'slut'. Feeling a little too exposed I quickly cover myself with the sheet...I'm clearly being punished for being disloyal to Ryan. But let's face it taking into account my past dating history, I can't really be blamed for keeping all my options open. Sylvia's mouth twitches as she's about to speak;

'I've read your notes, I see you fell…I'm not surprised wearing shoes like that.'

She's as cold as I remember her and in a panic I say the first thing that comes into my head;

'How's Josh, has he left home yet?'

Her breathing starts to get heavier, I've obviously pissed her off;

'Joshua is fine thank you. He's seeing a lovely girl, she's friend of the family so I know exactly where she's been. They are very happy, so don't you even think about contacting him again…ever!'

Poor Josh, he's royally fucked with Sylvia for a Mother, I just hope one day he grows the balls to walk out of the door and never go back. As for his poor girlfriend, I wish her all the luck in the world…she's going to need it. I decide not to say anything else and feel distinctly uncomfortable as Sylvia checks my eyes, I'm face to face with my nemesis and I feel like she's looking into my soul. She quickly scribbles something in my notes, tells me the nurse will give me a leaflet on head injuries and discharges me. Just as she turns to leave Ryan gets back with his drink, she looks at him menacingly and as she passes him whispers through gritted teeth;

'Is she with you? Be careful, she's a slut.'

Ryan is furious and is about to challenge her when I tell him not to bother, I explain that I went on a date with a guy who had the most frightening, over bearing Mother I had ever met. The date was a disaster culminating in me making a rapid escaped from a raging Sylvia who wasn't prepared to share her son with anyone. He laughs and tells me I haven't had much luck…he doesn't know the fucking half of it! I grab the head injury leaflet from the nurse and leave the hospital as quickly as I can. I'm a little disappointed that I didn't get to see Dr Gorgeous, but Ryan more than make up for it. He takes me back to mine where he tucks me up in bed and is more than happy to oblige when I ask him to join me. Neither of us are feeling particularly like doing anything other than sleep, so that's what we do. I spend the rest of the night and most of the morning asleep in Ryan's arms. I think I have finally done it, I've found my Mr Romance and my Mr Uninhibited rolled into one. I feel happy and content and I'm going to enjoy the moment as long as it lasts.

CHAPTER NINE

More lessons learnt

I haven't been around much the past few weeks, I've been spending more and more time at Ryan's. I'm loved up, happy and pleased to say my sex drought finally came to an end a couple of nights after I hurt my head. Ryan had popped over to mine with a chocolate hamper…yes he is fucking perfect. He blamed himself for me falling over, he felt that if he hadn't of asked me to keep my shoes on it wouldn't have happened. He's quite right but I won't hold it against him! I wasn't expecting him when he arrived and answered the door wearing nothing but towel as I had just had a bath. Naturally I was delighted to see him and even more delighted with the chocolate! He stepped into the house and shut the door behind him. As he reached down to kiss me my towel fell down, I didn't make any attempt to hide my nakedness, this was my one shot as getting a shag and I was going to take it. I took the chocolate hamper out of his hands and unceremoniously threw it into the living room. Then I pulled him down to the floor, unzipped his trousers and he fucked me there and then. No props, no erotic tricks just a good old fashioned shag. It didn't last long and there was no earth shattering orgasm but it was lovely and it was a start. I'm also pleased to report there were no pints of Guinness involved in any way whatsoever!

So what else have I learnt from my latest (and hopefully last) attempts at online dating. Firstly and this is quite important. If you ever keep a souvenir from a date, hide it somewhere nobody will ever find it…not in the tea towel drawer in your kitchen. If it hadn't have been Tom who had found it, it could have been my Mother and that would have involved a whole new level of explaining myself. Maybe it was for the best that Tom found Daniel's wax bellend. Firstly, said bellend is now destroyed and I won't ever have to worry about anyone finding it again and secondly, if Tom hadn't of dumped me I would never have met Ryan. Tom was lovely but I don't think it would have lasted, I think I'm much better suited to Ryan…he's definitely 'the one'. I know I said Tom was 'the one' but a lady is entitled to change her mind isn't she? Next, love balls are an interesting idea. To be honest they didn't do all that much for me, once I got it into my head that my fanny sounded like a walking wind chime I just didn't feel it. Whatever you do, and I can't stress this enough always read the instructions. Why the fuck did I not read the instructions and how stupid was I to actually think it was a good idea to insert the string as well? Just spending two minutes reading the instructions would have saved me the humiliation of having to have them manually removed, if it wasn't for the fact I got to see Dr Gorgeous it would have been a total disaster.

   Never trust a man who uses a black and white photograph on his dating profile, okay, maybe that's taking it a bit far as some people do prefer black and white pictures, but be wary. I thought Stanley was an enigmatic, arty type using a black and white photo for dramatic effect…he was a fucking pensioner! I thought I was doing my bit for the community by spending the evening with him, I thought he was a sweet, lonely old man when in reality he was a lecherous, dick pic sending philanderer…so never judge a book by its cover. All men are capable of lying, when Stanley should have been spending the autumn years of his life with his loyal and long suffering wife, he was prowling dating sites looking for a younger model…twat. What have I learnt from pretending Stanley was my Dad in order to spend time with Daniel…absolutely nothing. I hold my hands up, it was wicked and I am most likely going to hell, but it did mean I got to spend little bit of time with the delectable Daniel. Give me a break, I was mourning the loss of his wax bellend and spending a bit of time with him gave me closure.

   The countryside is a very dangerous place! Not only is it

an empty wilderness, there are cows everywhere. They are wandering around like they own the place, shitting where they feel like and if they get close to you they will try and eat you…that may sound over dramatic but I'd love to know how you'd feel if you woke up to a cow happily licking your ear lobe. Which leads me to never trust a man who loves the countryside, one minute he's romancing you with a fancy picnic, the next he's driving down a remote country lane so you can join the local dogging club. No fucking way, the cheeky bastard, what made him think I'd want to have sex with random strangers? He could have asked me, given me a choice but he so arrogant to think I was just going to go for it. What did he expect me to say?

'Oh Andrew, thank you so much for giving me the opportunity to have sex with Kev, Bob and Trev from the Farmer's Arms. I've never seen them before in my life but I'm more than happy to open my legs for them.'

'A mask, thank you so much! I always wanted to hide my face whilst having sex with strangers.'

'Dogging how charming, of course I'll give it a go.'

Cheeky twat! I didn't really understand it to be honest, Andrew was good looking, intelligent, funny…he could have had anyone he wanted, but preferred anonymous group sex. If you're on a date in the heart of the countryside and the man you are with suddenly hands you a mask…run a mile.

Roller skating is fun! Never let demons from your past stop you do anything. I was wary of going to the Roller Disco because it brought back memories of Julie Rigby and the cool girls at school, but I did it, I enjoyed it and I was actually quite good at it. I may not have had pink laces but I rocked the rink! Never have a bath in a hurry and leave the house with water in your ear, temporary deafness can cause all sorts of misunderstandings and you may end up getting a lifetime ban from your local Chinese restaurant. I've replayed that conversation with Ethan in my head a hundred times and although I struggled to hear what he was saying I was completely oblivious to some of the terminology he was using, I definitely need to have another look at the Urban Dictionary at some point. Don't be fooled by a sweet, nerdy man. Ethan looked like butter wouldn't melt in his mouth and I really thought that despite the fact I towered over him we got on well. But no, he sacked me off, thought I was nothing more than friend material. When push came to shove he just wasn't prepared to give me a chance. Would I have let him bash my back doors in? A lady never tells, so you'll just have to keep wondering about that one.

Don't live in the past. I fucked up with Daniel, I fucked up with his wax bellend and I should have accepted it was never going to happen and moved on. But I clung on to the hope that one day we would be reunited and I could continue my erotic adventure with him…for fucks sake, I only met him once, I really don't know why he impacted me so much. Anyway, it was never going to happen, he was just being polite in the pub when Stanley had his heart attack, doing what any good friend would. The dream I had was amazing and at least now I know what a Hollywood Wax is, but it showed me that it was unhealthy to keep chasing the impossible. It was time to let go of the Daniel fantasy, whilst I was still longing for a second chance, no one was going to be able to compete and I was stopping myself from being happy. Miss Fucking Perfection Personified was obviously his new girlfriend and there was no way I could compete with her. Daniel called me to see how my imaginary Dad was, but that was it. He wasn't going to call again, he had moved on. I was just a distant, probably quite bad memory to him and there was never going to be a repeat performance, even if I did promise to get rid of all the candles in my house. Daniel was an experience, part of life's rich tapestry. I didn't really know him and you now what, I bet he wasn't all that perfect…nobody is.

Never do anything you don't want to, I hate horror films but to impress Ryan I didn't tell him. If I'm honest the film was shit, cheesy shlock horror with no story or direction, but that's what some people love about horror movies. If I'd been straight up with Ryan I would have saved myself the embarrassment of nearly fainting at the sight of fake blood and the couple behind us would have been saved from being showered in popcorn. That said, if I hadn't of nearly fainted, he wouldn't have taken me home and we might not be where we are today. I found being drawn naked totally empowering, I was living my best erotic life and have been immortalised in pencil. It could be a bit awkward when I finally get to meet his parents, can you imagine we'll be drinking tea and making small talk in the shadow of my tits and muff. Maybe I'll ask him to take it down when I meet them. If something seems good, don't be too suspicious. It's just possible that everything is above board. Spying on Ryan and ending up face first in a bush was a bit of a low point, but like I said at the time it was only to be expected that I was going to be suspicious. All my dates prior to this had been such a disaster I was guilty of assuming Ryan was messing me around.

Doreen…what a woman! She's living proof that it's never too late. She's been in touch since she went on her cruise, apparently Stanley was furious but she stood her ground and currently she's somewhere in the Atlantic Ocean making up for all those lost years. Forty years she put up with Stanley's infidelity, forty years of not being cherished and yes she should have left sooner, but she's going to make up for it now. I'm definitely going to take her advice on board and do what makes me happy. Why should I conform to other people's ideas of what I should and shouldn't do…I've tried conforming to the rules of erotica and look where that's got me! For now Ryan is making me happy and I'm going to enjoy ever minute of it. Meeting Doreen was an education, who knew old ladies swore so much, I don't know why but I always imagined that by the time you turned fifty a swearing filter switched on and you would never utter and expletive again.

Shoes….fucking shoes! I knew I struggled to walk in three inch stilettos, so what the fuck possessed me to go for six inches? I mean they did look good and they turned Ryan on, but they were a danger to my health. Looking back I can see it was never going to end well, I'm naturally clumsy and should just stick to flats. Although I did manage to do the whole evening without falling over, the fact they let me down when I was within a cock's length of getting a shag made me hate them, so as soon as Ryan left the next day I bid the shoes a not so fond farewell and threw them in the bin. I need to go with what I'm comfortable with, not what I think makes me an erotic goddess. I'm sure if I greeted Ryan completely naked apart from my pink trainers he would find that erotic. I think I've come to the conclusion that erotica is what you make it and not what the books tell you. Finally…Dr Gorgeous. I'm with Ryan now so I really need to get Dr Gorgeous out of my head. I know nothing about him apart from he is actually gorgeous with a smile to die for. He has a lovely bedside manner and always manages to put me at ease no matter what predicament I've got myself into. But now I know Sylvia is lurking around the hospital I am going to do everything I can to avoid it, which means I probably won't see Dr Gorgeous again…he might be happily married for all I know, so I think now is a good time to put that particular fantasy to bed.

So where does that leave me? After more dating disasters than I'd care to remember, I'm blissfully happy with Ryan, we've only been together for a few weeks but so far things are looking wonderful. He's kind, thoughtful and has a brilliant personality, it's a huge bonus that he's also incredibly good looking and is he good in bed? That's for me to know and you to never to find out! My membership of the dating site has been cancelled, hopefully for good this time and my Ann Summers Rep hasn't heard from me for ages, her dildo sales must be well down! I've deleted Daniel's number from my phone and I'm more than ready to move on. I know nothing in life is certain, but I think I finally have my happy ending. Keep your fingers crossed!

Book 3

FLAMINGOS, FEARS & HAPPY TEARS

CHAPTER ONE

Ryan – lying, cheating shit

For the past six months I had been in a proper, grown up relationship with Ryan. I was content and so happy. He was nearly everything I could have wished for, he ticked all the boxes for my Mr Romance, but after a great start the sex became unspectacular. Ryan certainly couldn't be described as Mr Uninhibited. If anything, it was all about satisfying his needs and I had to make do with digging out and dusting off my Ann Summers stash. I had tried to spice things up on numerous occasions…the man just never got the hint. I could channel my inner erotic goddess and present myself to him in all manner of positions but he'd still flip me over into the missionary position, give me a good old pounding then roll over and go to sleep. I'd managed to perfect my 'oh Ryan, you're the King' orgasm face…he may have been shit, but I didn't want to hurt his feelings. At the end of the day, the sex was regular, loving and familiar and I had begun to accept that as a lover he was never going to set the world or my fanny on fire. Despite this, things had started to get really serious. I'd met his parents and he'd given me a key to his place. We'd spend evenings snuggled up on the sofa discussing baby names…he wanted Vincent (after Vincent Van Gogh) for a boy and I had chosen Kitty for a girl. I'd put my friends on bridesmaid alert and had started looking at wedding dresses. Once we'd hit the sixth month mark, I have to admit things had felt a little different, Ryan had started to become a bit distant, cancelling dates, not turning up when he said he would. I put it down to him quitting his job and working on his art full time. He'd taken a huge step and that was bound to be stressful. I would never have imagined what was going to happen on that fateful afternoon.

I had taken the afternoon off work and decided to surprise Ryan, I thought an al fresco afternoon shag might spice things up a bit. He definitely looked like he needing cheering up and I was just the girl to do it. I let myself in and could hear Ryan grunting in the sitting room, I didn't think anything of it as he was probably painting and it wasn't unusual to hear him huffing and puffing as he immersed himself in creativity. My fanny was starting to tingle as I opened the sitting room door. Ryan was incredibly attractive with an almost perfect physique and I never gave up hope that one day he would ravish me. I imagined his face when he saw me standing there and hoped he'd be so excited he might finally let me go on top for a change! When I opened the door, the first thing I noticed was the painting hanging over the fire place, there was definitely something familiar about it but it wasn't me…unless I suddenly dyed my hair blonde, had my lips plumped up and grown a pair of absolutely fucking huge tits! I was confused and was trying to rationalise why my painting had gone when I looked over the sofa and there was Ryan…balls deep in Miss Fucking Perfection Personified!

'Ryan…what the fuck!'

The colour drained from his face as he jumped up from the sofa covering his crotch as if I was a stranger. Miss Fucking Perfection Personified looked smug and not one bit sorry for destroying my life.

'Ann, I'm so sorry. You shouldn't have found out like this. I was going to tell you tonight that I didn't think things were working out.'

'Who the fuck is this Ryan?'

'Camilla's Dad owns an Art Gallery and we met when I took some of my paintings in to show him, I'm so sorry Ann.'

So Miss Fucking Perfection Personified was actually a posh bitch with a rich, art gallery owing Daddy. I couldn't compete with that could I? Why wasn't she with Daniel, why had she impacted my life yet again…I had to ask'.

'Camilla you absolute fucking bitch, I thought you were

with Daniel?'

'With who? Oh yes, Daniel…far too nice for me I found him terribly dull. Not at all like Ry Ry.'

Daniel…dull? Fucking Ry Ry! That was it, I couldn't contain myself any longer. I flung myself over the sofa and grabbed her by her perfectly coifed hair. She screamed as I grabbed her and Ryan screamed as he pulled me off and realised I had a handful of her hair extensions in my hand. I may have unruly curly hair that resembles my muff more than I'd care to admit, but at least it's all my own;

'Ha! Even your fucking hair is false. What's wrong with you, can't you get a boyfriend of your own, or do you just get a kick out taking someone else's man?'

'Ann, it's not Camilla's fault. I made all the first moves…there was something about her. I just couldn't resist.'

I couldn't believe what I was hearing, he actually went out of his way to get into Camilla's knickers even though he was with me…what a twat. By this point, I'd heard enough. I pulled his house keys out of my band flung them at him;

'Here's your keys Ryan. Why don't you shove them up your arse sideways, you utter utter cunt.'

With that I spun around and headed for the door;

'…and you were shit in bed.'

I looked at him for one last time and was pleased to see his face drop when I mentioned his performance or lack of in the bedroom. As I left I heard Camilla comforting him; 'Don't worry Ry, Ry you honestly gave me the best two minutes of my life earlier.'

Fucking two minutes…he was spoiling her!

As I slammed the door on the way out it felt like I was slamming the door on my future. Everything I had planned and believed in was gone.

So here I am alone again, Ryan has messaged me a couple of times…he's sorry, he didn't mean to hurt me…what utter bullshit he knew exactly what he was doing. I deleted his messages and blocked his number, I never want to hear from the cheating twat again. It's not long until Christmas and I'm destined to spend it with my Mum and Dad yet again. There'll be no quick shag under the Christmas tree…just dry turkey ,the Queen's speech and my Dad telling endless stories of Christmas in the 1950's…oh the fucking joy! My friends have been brilliant, we've shared many a bottle of Prosecco and I think I've bored them shitless talking about the wedding I was never going to have. They have hugged me when I have cried and given me a kick up the arse when I've needed it. I need to get back on the dating horse, apparently I'm getting on a bit and time is not on my side, which is not really what I wanted to hear but I suppose they do have a point. Unfortunately I don't think I will ever trust a man again and I really should have stuck to my original plan…just a good hard fuck and maybe a cup of coffee in the morning. So no more Mr Romance for me, it's going to be Mr Uninhibited all the way! I am Ann without an 'e' a liberated, erotic goddess looking for no strings sex. If you are looking for love, don't bother to apply.

It's been a couple of weeks since I split up with Ryan and I'm starting to feel better. I'm ready to move on. I am going to be in control from now on, mistress of my own destiny. Having had plenty of time to think about where I've been going wrong, I've decided I need to be more Camilla…she's obviously doing something right, she dated and dumped the delectable Daniel and then seduced Ryan. So in my quest to become a Camillaesque erotic goddess I'm waiting to have my first ever spray tan. I feel quite excited and I got a really good deal because a trainee is doing it. The beauty therapist calls me into the tanning booth and hands me what looks like paper serviette;

'If you could take everything off and put these on I'll be back in a couple of minutes.'

It takes me a few seconds to register she's given me a pair of paper knickers…I'm horrified, my muff only does cotton!

But if wrapping my fanny up like a takeaway kebab is what I need to do in my quest to become an erotic goddess then so be it. I step into the booth slightly concerned the paper knickers aren't going to be able to contain my arse when the therapist starts to spray...shit that's cold! I follow her instructions, I turn to the side, lift up my arms and open my legs. When it comes to her spraying the back of my legs, she makes sure to fill in my stretch marks which is a relief as I was slightly concerned I may end up looking like an orange zebra. Spray tan done, I get dressed and feel slightly damp and squishy. I have a quick look in the mirror and I am definitely glowing, I have to wait for a few hours before I have a bath so my tan can develop but it's looking good so far. As I'm walking home, I notice I do get a few looks...it's working already, my tanned healthy glow is turning heads...fuck you Camilla!!

When I get home I make myself a well deserved cup of coffee, I'm moving on and I'm proud of myself. I've been home about half an hour when I have a look in the mirror...fuck me! I don't look brown, glowing or healthy. I am bright neon orange! Why the hell did I agree to let a trainee do my tan? She must have used the wrong strength of tanning lotion because I make an orange look pale and I'm not exaggerating to say I look like an Oompa Loompa...I may as well give Willy Wonka a call because no other fucker is going to be interested in me looking like this. I wasn't getting looks on the way home because I look irresistible, people were looking at me because I look like the Tango man's love child. I quickly run a hot bath and I'm not getting out until I'm at least four shades lighter.

Two hours and lots of scrubbing later I am an acceptable shade of orange. This being glamorous business is hard work and I'm not sure I can be arsed! I've decided to set up my online dating profile again and I need to do some new photographs, a fresh start needs fresh pictures. I decide to go for the doe-eyed pouty look which I had previously rejected, yes it does make me look pissed but it seems to be popular. Maybe if I tone it down a bit I'll look less inebriated. Fabulous, the more subtle pouty look actually seems to work and my photos look quite good. I upload them to my profile and I'm ready to go…again. It's not long before my phone pings with a notification…I'm fully anticipating a dick pic but I'm pleasantly surprised to see it's a message from Alex. He's the same age as me and looks very nice. I message him back straight away, I don't care if I look too keen…I'm taking control is my new mantra. After about an hour of exchanging flirty messages we agree to meet;

'I'm really looking forward to seeing you Ann and I've

been thinking about what we could get up to. Are you into water sports?'

Am I into water sports? Not really, I got my 5m swimming badge at school and I don't mind a paddle in the sea but that's about it. Water sports means water skiing, surfing and water polo…doesn't it? It might be fun so I quickly hop onto my laptop and order a wet suit whilst still messaging Alex on my phone;

'I love water sports, will I need to bring my wet suit?'

'Sure, I've never tried it with a wet suit myself, but go ahead, it might add a little something'

'Add a little something?' He must be proper hard core if he does his water sports without a wet suit, I wonder if there's anywhere I can get water skiing lessons before I meet him.

'Alex, just so I know what else I need to bring with me, what kind of water sports are you into?'

'Just golden showers Ann, is there something else you're into?'

Golden showers? What the fuck is that…snorkelling in the sunlight? I suddenly get a sinking feeling in my stomach and quickly have a look at the Urban Dictionary on my laptop…Golden showers, the act of…absolutely no way, not happening! The last person that peed on me was my cousin's three month old baby…I'm sorry Alex it's just a big no from me. I don't know what to say, so I just say the first thing that comes into my head;

'Sorry Alex got to go…my cat just died and I think I'm going to be unavailable for a bit…bye.'

With that, I deleted his messages and took a deep breath…shit! What the fuck was that all about? Do you think I'll be able to get my money back on the wet suit I just bought?

Just as I'm thinking it wasn't a good idea to get back into online dating my phone pings with another message…this must be a record, no dick pics and two men interested in my profile within a couple of hours of each other. I feel like I can't be arsed after the conversation I've just had, but my curiosity gets the better of me. The message is from Leo, he's 35 and a plumber (oh the irony). He's very attractive and I might just be tempted to message him back.

CHAPTER TWO

Leo

I did it, I messaged Leo back and I'm going to give him a try. I can't wait to see him in the flesh. He's extremely fit with blonde curly hair and dark brown eyes. He looks like he could be a bit of a charmer…that's fine by me, I'm not after a life partner just a good shag and a handshake in the morning. I'm meeting him today and we're going to the beach…the beach in the middle of fucking winter, what on earth was I thinking? I would say it's quite romantic, but that romance nonsense is not for me any more. After Ryan I took all my romance novels to the charity shop, let some other poor deluded soul read them. Mr Romance is dead, long live Mr Uninhibited! I had thought about messaging Daniel, after all he had been dumped too, but I decided against it…Daniel is ancient history and there's no way I want Camilla's sloppy seconds. I imagine her talking to Ryan after I left;

'Don't worry Ry, Ry. She'll be fine, she'll just go straight back to Daniel.'

She's very much mistaken if she thinks Daniel would ever date me again… I suppose she doesn't know the history of Daniel's bellend. It left him so mentally scarred that every time he lays eyes on me he all he sees is his smouldering penis. Do I wish Ryan every happiness in his new relationship - do I fuck, I hope she tramples all over his heart like he trampled over mine! Enough of Ryan, I need to focus on my date with Leo…look forward not back. It's so cold today, I don't think I'll be unleashing my inner erotic goddess as the tide rolls in so I opt for comfort and lots of layers. My chunky cream jumper shows of my toned down tan to perfection and I've put my hair up…I can't be arsed with the windswept look today…windswept conjures up a vision of romance to me and I am not fucking going there. A quick spray of perfume and a coat of lipstick and I'm ready to go. So here I am, back on the dating horse, I just hope I get ridden like one!

I head off to meet Leo and still can't quite believe I agreed to go to the beach in sub- zero temperatures. I must be desperate, let's face it, I am a bit…desperate for a decent shag. We are meeting on the promenade next to a fresh donut stall, I'm grateful for the heat coming off the fryer and the donuts smell so absolutely divine I can't resist the temptation. I'm a bit early so a quick sugary donut before he arrives won't do me any harm. They are delicious and so moreish one donut soon turns into three. They are so tasty and remind me of my childhood, of hot summer days spent at the beach. It's quite comforting in the cold and as I'm relishing the final one when I see Leo striding purposefully towards me, he smiles and waves;

'Hey Ann.'

I can't respond my mouth is full of donut and I'm covered in sugar, he's getting closer and I'm chewing as quickly as I can, but it just won't go down. I look like a sugar covered hamster and it's not a good look. There's only one thing for it, I quickly turn around and spit it out. As soon as it hits the ground it's spotted by hungry seagulls who descend on my feet, I'm tripping over them as I try to make my way towards Leo…the evil fuckers are squawking and flapping around my legs for more. There's one (I'm guessing the alpha seagull) which is staring me down, it's tapping at my shoes for more…the cheeky fucker. I'm getting flustered as I'm trying to look sexy and seductive as I lick the sugar off my lips, battling angry seagulls is not the look I was aiming for;

'Why don't you just FUCK OFF! Sorry Leo, not you…the seagulls, the seagulls can fuck off.'

Leo throws his head back and roars with laughter as he watches me trying to fend off the angry birds. Like a true gentleman he shoos them away;

'Get away, shoo…leave her lovely feet alone.'

That sounds promising, he even thinks my feet are lovely;

'Are you ok Ann? They didn't scratch your feet did they? He's so concerned, I might be in here!

We go for a short walk along the promenade and Leo suggests we head down to the beach. It's fairly deserted as most people are sensible enough avoid the seaside when it's wet and cold…what the hell am I doing? We walk for a bit and I must admit even though it's cold the beach does bring out the child in me. I'm happily collecting shells and hopping over rock pools when Leo suggests we take out shoes off so we can feel the sand between our toes. The adult in me thinks 'are you mad, it's fucking freezing.' My inner child however, is well up for it! I take my shoes and socks off and feel the cold sand between my toes. I notice Leo hasn't taken his own shoes off and he also hasn't taken his eyes off my feet…I think he's still a little worried that the mad seagulls took a bite out of me;

'What does the sand between your toes feel like Ann?'

What on earth does he expect me to say? It feels like sand. Has he never felt the sand between his toes before, does he have some kind of sand allergy? I don't want to offend him just in case he's had some sort of traumatic sand episode so I describe it the best I can;

'It just feels like sand really, cold, slightly damp and a bit gritty.'

He seems quite happy with my explanation and smiles contentedly as we carry on walking down the beach. We're chatting away like we've known each other for years, we have the same taste in music and films and his cheeky smile is definitely starting to make my fanny tingle. We come to some steps and decide to sit down, I stretch my legs and wiggle my bare toes;

'Just stay like that Ann, it would make a gorgeous photo.'

He wants to take a photo of me mid-stretch? Whatever turns him on! As he points his phone at me to take the picture I give him my most seductive smile. Hang on, he seems to be pointing the camera at my feet and taking multiple pictures…this is strange, why the fuck is he taking pictures of my feet? Maybe he's got a new fangled phone where you don't have to point it directly at the subject, yes that's what it will be it. I'm so behind when it comes to technology. It's getting colder so I put my shoes and socks back on…Leo looks strangely disappointed but at least my feet are warm. We get up and start walking along the beach again. Leo picks up a piece of driftwood and writes my name in the sand…hmm, we're bordering on romantic here. Not wanting to go down the romance route, I take the driftwood off him and draw the first thing that comes to mind…a huge cock. Leo looks, stops and then bursts out laughing. We also seem to share the same sense of humour…I get the feeling Leo might actually be the Mr Uninhibited I've been looking for.

We've been walking for what seems like miles when we come across some more rock pools;

'Why don't you have a paddle Ann?'

Because it's fucking freezing! What on earth is he thinking, does he want me to get frost bite? I politely decline, explaining that I don't have a towel so wouldn't be able to dry my feet. In a flash he opens up his rucksack and produces a fluffy blue towel…what the fuck? I suppose it's sensible to take a towel to the beach, but in the middle of winter, really? He clearly wants me to have the full beach experience and it's not like he's asked me to go skinny dipping so I take off my socks and shoes and start to paddle;

'Shit, Leo it's so cold!'

'You'll soon get used it, just paddle around a bit and maybe splash the water with your toes.'

This is getting stranger and stranger. As I'm paddling around I notice he has his phone out and he's pointing it at me feet again. I'm sure there's an innocent explanation, maybe he's into nature and spotted a rare starfish in the rock pool. Honestly though, it's starting to feel a bit uncomfortable so I tell Leo I've had enough;

'It's too cold, I'm coming out. I'm not sure it's healthy to paddle in the winter.'

He gets the towel ready and as I sit down, rather than hand it to me he starts to dry my feet. He rubs my feet really slowly and he seems to relishing every second of it. If I'm honest I would say he was getting turned on, when he starts to rub them more quickly I snatch the towel off him;

'It's alright Leo, I can dry them myself.'

He looks disappointed again as I finish drying my feet myself. I quickly put my shoes and socks back on and he's watching my every move. We start to head back to the promenade and Leo is chatting enthusiastically…about my feet. Apparently they are perfect, my toes are delicate and my nail to toe ratio is excellent. What do I say to that?

'Leo I'm thrilled you are happy with the distance between my little and big toes.'

'Now you've seen my feet would you like to see my tits?'

'No you can't suck my toes in public.'

I'm starting to come to the realisation that Leo is only interested in me below the knees. He's less a pint of Guinness and a quick shag and more a pint of Guinness and a quick look at your feet. We get back to the donut stall where we first met and I wonder whether we will go on another date…do I want to go on another date?

'It was so good to meet you Anne, I'll message you and

maybe we'll meet up again…next time maybe you could wear a nice pair of strappy heels.'

With that he left. No kiss goodbye, no flirty wave, he just fucked of without so much as a second glance. It's all become clear to me now, he has a foot fetish…he must have! All those photos he took, he's going to be wanking over them later. Cheeky bastard, dragging me out in the freezing cold, subjecting me to a crazed seagull attack, all because he wanted to get some photographs of my feet and as for the strappy heels, he can shove those…maybe I should get a toe ring or a foot thong? Where would it end, would he want a toe up the arse? He's got no chance! I had high hopes for Leo. I was attracted to him, he made my fanny tingle but I need someone who is interested in my whole body…that's not too much to ask is it?

I call my friend Veronica when I get home. She can barely talk for laughing when I tell her about my foot date from hell;

'Fucking hell Ann, you don't have much luck do you love?'

Talk about stating the obvious! When it comes to the opposite sex I am seriously cursed. At least I'm laughing, I shed so many tears over Ryan it's nice to be able to smile again and she's organising a blind date for me. How exciting, I've never been on a blind date before and as I don't seem to be having much success (no success) with online dating I may as well give it a go. She has a work colleague who has had a series of failed relationships (sounds familiar) and he's looking to meet someone. He's called Joe and he's 31. Veronica can't speak highly enough about him. He's funny, clever and very charming apparently. She's going to message him now and try and organise something.

Waiting, waiting, waiting...it's been over an hour and Veronica hasn't called me back. Maybe he's had second thoughts or maybe she let slip that I burn bellends. Just as my thoughts turn to joining a nunnery in a remote highland village she calls back;

'Hi love, it's on!.'

How exciting, I'm going on my first ever blind date. I'm meeting Joe tomorrow, we're going for a drink at the White Hart pub. I'm to wait at the bar and wear a green scarf so he knows it's me. Shit, do I even have a green scarf? I'll need to pop into town on my lunch break tomorrow and pick one up. I haven't got a clue what Joe looks like but he's also going to be wearing a green scarf so if he's over sixty I'll be able to identify him a run. As I'm getting ready for bed my phone pings with a message from the dating site. I'm not going to bother looking at it, I'll see how things go with Joe. I may be an erotic goddess in training but two men on the go is too much for me…especially with my track record.

CHAPTER THREE

Joe

I'm nearly ready for my blind date with Joe. I follow my usual routine of a long hot bath, exfoliation and muff trim. I call it a trim, but my poor lady garden had been so neglected since I split up with Ryan that it was completely out of control. I had more bush than the Chelsea Flower Show, it was so unruly I wasn't sure whether I was going to need scissors or gardening shears. I'm wearing a short woolly dress with a polo neck and thick tights…I may be an erotic goddess but it's too fucking cold to get my tits out! I've straightened my hair and in an attempt to become more Camilla, I bought some clip-in hair extensions…I can't do the huge boobs or big pouty lips but at least I can do the long flowing locks and I still have my tan.

I'm waiting in the pub to meet Joe, I'm early as usual…I might be shit at dating but at least I'm punctual. I finally managed to get a green scarf, what a faff that was. It took me ages to find one, I'm guessing green scarves aren't the 'in' thing this winter. I decided to wear flat shoes just in case I have to make a quick getaway and I've also made sure I'm standing right in front of the fire exit. I'm watching the doors, waiting for joe…I'm excited but also a little anxious. I thought I was going to be with Ryan forever and now here I am dating again…I feel like a novice, what if I never meet anyone to spend the rest of my life with? What if I'm alone for so long my muff heals? Ok, so I know that's not going to happen but I don't want to be on my own. I quickly give myself a kick, this is not operation find a husband, it's operation get a long hard shag. The pub doors swing open and an attractive women walks in, she's wearing a green scarf (it has a couple of yellow lines running through it, but it's still green) and I wonder whether Joe has double booked…wouldn't that be typical. She's followed by a man wearing a green scarf and I wonder whether he's Joe, he looks me in the eyes and completely ignores me so I'm guessing it's not. The doors open again and a group of about eight people walk in, they are all wearing green scarves. What the fuck is going on? It doesn't take long for me to realise as on the wall behind me is a huge 'School Reunion' banner. For fucks sake, how am I going to recognise Joe? Every fucker is wearing a green scarf in here.

Just as I'm considering going home, the pub door swings open again and in walks an absolute man mountain. He's so tall and so muscular and to my absolute delight he's walking straight towards me;

'You must be Ann?'

Happy fucking days! This is Joe, Veronica described me to him so along with the green scarf (which I will now treasure forever) he knew exactly who I was. I can't take my eyes off him, he looks like a Greek God. We find a table away from the school reunion, I've already been asked if I'm Anita, Karen or Tracey and I can't be arsed explaining I'm here for a shag, not to reminisce about the time Billy Robinson called the maths teacher a slag and stormed out of the classroom. Thankfully because we have a mutual friend the conversation between me a Joe is flowing. Veronica was right, he is hilarious, I haven't laughed so much in ages. Everything about him is perfect, how the hell is he still single? I think he could be interested and he hasn't looked at my feet once. Every time he makes eye contact with me my fanny doesn't just tingle, it feels like its going to explode. The pub is starting to get quite rowdy as the school reunion is in full swing, a bloke standing next to our table burps loudly in our direction and Joe looks horrified and I'm sure he's gone a bit pale. We finish our drinks and he suggests we go and get a curry, I'm not sure if he's hungry or if he's so disgusted by the burping guy he just wants to leave. Either way I'm delighted that the evening's not ending.

As we are walking to the restaurant Joe puts one of his

huge, strong arms around my shoulders and I feel strangely content. We arrive and Joe is the perfect gentleman, opening the door for me and pulling out my chair so I can sit down. I can't get carried away, he does have the making of both my Mr Romance and my Mr Uninhibited but this has to be about sex, sex and more sex. I am not going to have my heart broken again. The waiter brings our menus and Joe asks what I would like, I haven't had a curry for ages so I tell him I'll have whatever he's having;

'Can I have two chicken vindaloo curries with pilau rice please.'

Did I hear right, did he just order me a chicken vindaloo? That's one of the hottest curries isn't it? I'll just have to try and impress him with my curry eating stamina…show him there's nothing I can't do. The waiter brings our food and just to remind me how hot the curry is actually going to be, he also brings a jug of water to the table. What the fuck have I done…I usually go for a chicken korma and even that makes my eyes water sometimes. Joe dives in straight away and he looks amused as I cautiously prod at my curry with some naan bread…I'm going to take this slowly;

'Do you not like the curry Ann? Go on…dig in.'

There's nothing else for it, I take a huge mouthful and hope for the best…fuck it's hot! I try to regain my composure as my tongue starts to burn. I smile and nod at Joe as finish my first mouthful. He knowingly pours me a glass of water and I drink it down in one;

'Is the curry too hot? Should I order you something else.'

'No, Joe it's fine. Absolutely delicious, I'm sure I'll get used to the heat.'

Why oh why, did I not ask him to order me an omelette? I carry on eating and I think my tongue must be numb as I'm getting used to the to heat. I eat about half and accept defeat;

'That was great Joe, but I had something to eat before I came out. I wasn't that hungry.'

He touches my hand and laughs, he knows I'm a curry wimp! Joe must have an asbestos tongue as he's finished his curry without flinching once…not only does he look like a Greek God he's a curry God too. We have ice-cream for dessert which was delightful and as we are drinking our coffee I feel Joe's hand on my knee, he starts to stroke my leg and my fanny is beside itself. I feel like dragging him into the nearest alleyway and letting him fuck me against the wall. I slip off my shoe and just as I'm about to start rubbing his crotch with my foot someone on the table next to us sneezes loudly. Joe looks absolutely appalled, takes his hand off my knee and calls the waiter over for the bill. I'm starting to think that even though Joe is a man mountain of biblical proportions, he is also a tad sensitive. Sensitivity isn't a bad thing, all men could do with embracing their sensitive side and it just makes Joe even more perfect.

Joe pays the bill (I did offer to pay half but he was having none of it) and we head outside to find a taxi. As we get outside, Joe sweeps me up into his arms and kisses me passionately…I wasn't expecting that, but it was very nice. I immediately take the initiative;

'Do you want to come to mine?'

'I'd love to Ann.'

Here we go, I think it's on…I'm going to give the big man the time of his life! We jump into a taxi and my tummy starts to feel strange, it's churning and grumbling. I knew I shouldn't have had that curry. As soon as we get back to mine I show Joe into the lounge and then I go into the kitchen and have a large glass of milk to try and settle my stomach. I open a bottle of wine and take it into the lounge where Joe is nearly taking up the whole sofa. As I'm taking in the vision in front of me it suddenly hits me…if he's that big, how big is his dick going to be? I hope it's not going to be a James mark two, I really don't think I'm up for a gargantuan cock tonight. I hand Joe a glass of wine and squeeze in next to him, he immediately puts the glass down and gently strokes my face;

'I've really enjoyed this evening Ann, you really are beautiful.'

My fanny is tingling and my stomach is grumbling…I hope he can't hear it, it really doesn't sound happy. He leans in and kisses me passionately, as he gets more excited he grabs my hair and to my absolute horror my hair extensions come off in his hand…I know I wanted to be more like Camilla, but this is not what I had in mind. He immediately stops kissing me and recoils in disgust as he looks at the hair in his hand;

'It's okay Joe, they are just hair extensions. I obviously didn't put them in right.'

He calms down as I explain, the poor man had the shock of his life. He's like a caramel toffee, hard on the inside and soft in the middle. He hands me back my hair and I chuck it over the back of the sofa…I need to work hard to get back on track now. I slide my hand up his thigh and I'm pleased to say his cock feels on the larger side but it's not so big I won't walk for a week after having sex. He starts to kiss me again, his tongue is probing my mouth purposefully and his hand has moved to between my legs…why the fuck did I put these thick tights on? He unzips my dress and I slip it over my head whilst also trying to pull my passion killing tights off. Joe gently pushes me back onto the sofa and starts kissing me working downwards from my neck. Before I know it he's unclipped my bra and he's teasing my nipple with his tongue. I guide his head downwards and he traces a line down my stomach with his tongue. As he reaches my belly button I can feel my stomach grumble, really grumble and then…..PAAAAAAARP! I don't know where it came from, but I did the loudest, longest fart I think I have ever heard. The colour drains from Joe's face and he jumps about six feet into the air as the sound of my fart reverberates around the room. Fucking hell, I don't know where to look or what to say. I scramble to put my dress back on as Joe flies towards the door;

'I'm so sorry Joe, I don't usually fart on a first date and I didn't follow through!'

'I didn't follow through' what the fuck was I thinking! Joe looks even more horrified;

'I'm going to have to go Ann, I'll be in touch.'

With that he lets himself out and I watch out of the window as he literally sprints down the road. Another dating disaster to add to the list. I'm not entirely to blame though, Joe did order me the hottest curry on the menu and he's so sensitive. If he doesn't like burping, farting and sneezing it would never have worked between us. Now I know why he's still single!

I'm just about to go to bed when I remember the message on my phone. Can I really be arsed? At this point, I feel I've got nothing to lose…I just farted on a first date, I don't think it could get worse than that. I open the message and it's from Luke, he's a chatty 36 year old engineer. He's written a very entertaining paragraph about himself. He likes dogs but thinks cats are twats…I agree. He's looking for an open minded lady who's up for a laugh…he could be talking about me and he thinks olives are the devil's work…a man after my own heart. Luke sounds fun, I bet he wouldn't have minded me farting at an inopportune moment! I message him back and go to bed waiting for his reply.

CHAPTER FOUR

Luke

Luke replied pretty much straight away and yesterday we met up for a quick coffee. He was the complete opposite to Joe…average height, average build and although not God like, he was pleasantly good looking with a mop of vibrant red hair. He was so funny, he made me laugh from the moment I sat down to the moment I left. He had no airs and graces and I really don't think he's offended by bodily functions. It turns out he went to school with my twat of a cousin Adrian…it's a small world! They were just in the same year, not friends which is a relief…now the handcuff joke is wearing a bit thin Adrian is looking for new dirt to dish on me. He was very sweet when we talked about what we were looking for in a relationship, he agreed with me that it should be fun all the way, but he also thought 'sharing was caring'…I'm assuming he means everything should be equal within a relationship which is fine by me. I am Ann without an 'e', erotic goddess and not beholden to anyone. We absolutely clicked and tomorrow we are going for a night away in what Luke described as an exclusive country house hotel. He's been the perfect gentleman and booked us separate rooms. If he's anything like he was on our coffee date, I don't think I'll be using my room much!

My bag is packed and I'm ready to go. We are going for a meal this evening so I've packed a pretty dark blue cocktail dress, it's about time I got my legs and cleavage out again. I wonder what the club is going to be like, it does sound posh…yet there's nothing posh or snobby about Luke at all. Whatever it's like I'm sure it's going to be fun. As I'm waiting for Luke, I can't help thinking about Joe, he hasn't been in contact since my trumping faux pas and I think it's safe to say I'm not going to be on his Christmas card list this year. I can hear a car beeping outside, it's Luke…here we go! I get into the car and Luke plants a kiss on my lips, he's obviously starting as he means to go on;

'Hey Ann, are you ready to have some fun?'

Too right I am, I shoot him a flirty look…well I think was flirty but it may well have been more squinty like I was struggling to see his face. He winks at me and puts the radio on, we end up singing along to every song together…I'm having fun already and we're only half an hour in! It's not long before we arrive, Luke pulls into the car park and it all looks lovely. The old country house is set in acres of countryside and if I wasn't anti-romance I would say it's quite romantic. Luke gets our bags out of the car and we go to check in. As we are waiting for our keys he tells me that the whole house has been given over to tonight's event…I have no idea what this event he's talking about is, but I do notice lots of boxes of tissues dotted around the place…maybe they're hosting a wankathon! Our rooms are next to each other which is quite sweet. My room is lovely, I've had the obligatory bounce on the bed and checked out the complimentary toiletries. To my surprise along with the small bottles of shampoo and shower gel there's also a packet of condoms…they clearly think of everything here. They'll definitely be getting a five star review when I get back, I'm most impressed. Luke knocks on my door and I let him in;

'What do you think of the room Ann, it's fab isn't it…you could easily fit six in here.'

He's clearly impressed that the rooms are spacious, but I think six is pushing it, there's not enough space for six beds. I don't want to dampen his enthusiasm so I agree with him;

'Oh yes, you could comfortably get six people in here.'

He looks strangely excited by this comment. He must be an interior design enthusiast…I'll ask him about that later. Luke kisses me again as he leaves my room, we're going down to dinner at 7pm so I have an hour to get ready.

I'm all ready and I have to admit I look hot…Luke is not

going to be able to resist me. My dress shows off a little bit of cleavage and a lot of leg. I've put my hair (minus hair extensions, they went straight in the bin) up in an attempt to look sophisticated and I don't think I could look anymore like an erotic goddess if I tried…I'm definitely giving the perfect Camilla a run for her money in this outfit. Right on time Luke knocks on my door;

'Wow Ann, you look stunning. We're going to be in demand tonight!'

What did he mean by that, why are we going to be in demand? Does he think we look like celebrities? The dining room is packed when we get down there, it's mainly couples but there are a few single diners. The waiter shows us to our table and hands us our menus;

'What do you fancy Ann, I'm going for the curry.'

Curry? No thank you! I opt for the grilled chicken, it's unexciting but at least I know it won't upset my stomach. Luke orders us a bottle of champagne and I'm feeling contented with the occasional fanny tingle thrown in for good measure. Luke is his chatty, funny self and everyone else in the dining room seems really friendly. We are getting lots of waves and winks from the other couples and a couple of people have popped over to say hello. Luke is being so attentive, he keeps telling me how lovely I look and how proud he is to be with me. I'm convinced it won't be long before I unleash my inner erotic goddess on him. We finish eating and Luke suggests we head down to the bar. I was hoping he's want to head back to my bedroom, but I can wait. We order some drinks and Luke heads towards another couple sitting on a sofa;

'Ann, I'd like you to meet Nigel and Gloria.'

I say hello and we shake hands, I didn't realise Luke had friends staying here. Nigel and Gloria look to be a more mature couple. Nigel can't take his eyes off my cleavage, it's slightly unnerving and when he goes to the bar I mention it to Luke;

'Nigel keeps looking at my tits the cheeky bastard.'

'It's because he can't wait to get his hands on them.'

That wasn't the answer I was expecting. Nigel was in for a long wait, it would be a cold day in hell before he was going to get his hands anywhere near my tits. I'm sure Luke was only joking and is secretly seething at his so called mate leching over me. At least Gloria seems nice, she's chatty and I think she can tell Nigel is freaking me out as she keeps trying to put me at ease;

'So is this your first time here Ann are you feeling a bit nervous?'

Nervous about what, coming to a hotel?

'No. I'm fine. I'm enjoying the evening, Luke is great company.'

'Yes, I agree Luke is fantastic.'

She winks at me and gives me a knowing look…surely she's not one of Luke's exes, she's old enough to be his Mother. This evening is starting to take a strange turn. I stand up and ask Luke for a quick word;

'Should we take the party elsewhere Luke?'

He looks absolutely fucking delighted! He tells me he has something to show me and starts to usher me towards another room. I look behind me and Nigel and Gloria are following us…fucking stalkers what's their problem, can't they tell we want to be alone. I ask Luke if we are going back upstairs;

'Later Ann, I want to show you the hot tub first.'

Hot tub? I haven't brought my swimming costume with me…shit! Luke flings open a set of double doors which leads to the hot tub room. I don't think I will ever be able to unsee what awaited me. There were at least eight people in the hot tub, all naked and all over each other…there were legs arms and cocks everywhere. On the sofas surrounding it there were at least two sets of couples sharing the fucking love…in front, underneath, behind. I felt like I was in that film The Human Centipede as it was hard to tell where one body finished and another one started. Suddenly one of the blokes in the hot tub looks at me and gestures me to get in…fuck off! I look behind me and Luke, Nigel and Gloria are already naked. I may be a bit slow on the uptake, but it finally hits me…he's brought me to a swingers hotel! I'm so stupid, he dropped enough hints 'sharing is caring', 'we are going to be in demand' and then there were the tissues everywhere…I was right, it is a wankathon of sorts. Luke jumps into the hot tub;

'Come on in Ann, the water is lovely.'

Of course it is…the water is steaming stew of bodily secretions and you couldn't pay me enough money to get in there;

'You're alright thanks Luke, why the fuck did you not tell me you were bringing me to a swingers night…you're not friends with Andrew by any chance are you?

'I thought you'd be up for it, come on give it a try…get your swinging wings.'

'Thanks, but no thanks. I like my men one at a time. Thanks for dinner, I'll make my own way home.'

As I turn around to flounce out I see a flash of pink in the corner of my eye. I look back and she's there, standing watching in the corner…the flamingo. She's staring at me intently and even though her face is covered by the flamingo mask, there's something familiar about her. I think she's see the flicker of recognition in my eyes as she quickly disappears into another room. I'm half tempted to follow her but fuck knows what I might see and I've had more than enough for one evening. I get back to my room, pack my bag and call a taxi...what a fucking evening. I need to change my dating profile when I get back...no swingers, doggers, hot wax, feet, horse whips, handcuffs, mothers or unfaithful shits!

I'm home, well that's another tale to tell the Grandchildren...or maybe not! I seriously am losing all faith in men, what's wrong with them? Where the fuck did Luke get off putting me in that situation without warning me, it's Andrew all over again...I've got a one man muff, how hard is that to understand? I pour myself a glass of prosecco and go outside for a cigarette, there's one thing that really is puzzling me though...who is the flamingo? There really was something about her that made me think I know her...could it be Camilla, she does seems to be following me around...if it was her does it mean she's left Ryan or was Ryan there somewhere? I'll probably never find out...the swinging flamingo is destined to be one of life's great mysteries! I check my phone as I had turned the notifications off when I was with Luke. I've got two dick pics and oh the joy, the marrow man is back, but this time he appears to have a butternut squash shoved where the sun don't shine. I delete the pictures and despair in my inability to get a good hard shag…am I destined to be a bitter old spinster who hates small children but loves small yappy dogs. I am a failed erotic goddess, how did the posh bird in 50 Shades do it?

After a restless nights sleep I wake up to two messages on my phone. One is from Leo, he's wondering when we can get together again as he can't get my beautiful feet out of his head…well he can fuck off and lust over someone else's feet…I'm a human being not an instep. The second is from someone on the dating site he's called Archie and he's really good looking and he looks very familiar. I take another look at his picture and still can't place him, I definitely know him…but who is he? Then it hits me…it's only Dr Gorgeous! I can't believe it, Dr Gorgeous is messaging me, I need to see what he has to say;

'Hi Ann, fancy seeing you here. I wondered if you'd like to meet up?'

Would I like to meet up? Hmm, let me think about that one…too fucking right I do! I don't want to look to keen so wait a whole five minutes before I message him back. I've invited him to come over to mine for a meal…shit, do I look too keen. It's not as if we haven't met and lets face it, he has already seen my fanny!

CHAPTER FIVE

Archie

I'm pleased to report Dr Gorgeous, sorry Archie is coming round tonight! I've a had a couple of days to prepare and the first thing I did was dig all my erotica novels out of the bin for a spot of revision. After the Luke incident, I threw them all away...the cheeky bastard never messaged me to apologise. Like Andrew, he probably got it on with the flamingo after I left. I really wish I knew who she was. It's been bugging me so much, there was something about her eyes and I just can't put my finger on it. I've got a bumper delivery coming this morning...a black basque and a little surprise for Archie. I've got a chicken casserole in my slow cooker (I am nothing if not organised) and I can spend the rest of the day transforming myself into a sexually liberated erotic goddess. I've got a good feeling about Archie, it feels like it was always meant to be and all the other disasters I've had were a practise run for the real thing.

I've spent the day reading and preparing for Archie. The postman came and gave me one of his cheeky knowing winks as he delivered my parcel, so I'm all set. The black basque is amazing, it perks my tits up no end and covers my arse to perfection and Archie is going to love his surprise. I'm wearing a shortish skirt and a low cut top…I've got to make the most of my enhanced cleavage after all. I've left my hair curly and my make up is natural. I'm nervous and excited at the same time and when the doorbell rings I nearly jump out of my skin. I compose myself and answer the door and there he is in all his glory…he's so handsome and with the winter sun shining behind him he looks like he's cloaked in a halo of light…he look almost biblical. He hands me a beautiful bunch of flowers and I feel myself go weak at the knees;

'Hi Ann, good to see you somewhere that's not the hospital.'

I giggle like a school girl and then blush with embarrassment as I remember he knows all my secrets! I show Archie into my lounge and grab a bottle of wine from the kitchen. I frantically search for a vase, but I don't think I've got one…I pop the flowers in a milk bottle and I'll just have to hope he doesn't notice. When I go back into the lounge Archie looks at home on my sofa and he's not so big that I have to squeeze in next to him. As we are chatting away, he suddenly mentions Sylvia;

'So how do you know Sylvia, I mentioned I was seeing you tonight and she wasn't all together complimentary.'

I explain about my date with Josh and how much she

disapproved of me, he laughs out loud when I tell him how she covered up my cleavage and chased me out of the house calling me a slut.

'That sounds like Sylvia, no woman will ever be good enough for her Joshy. I'm glad she put you off, if she didn't I wouldn't be here now.'

I start giggling again, did he really just say that? The idea of no strings attached sex and a brew in the morning has gone right out of the window. I'm thinking marriage, babies and a house in the countryside with donkeys in the garden.

I'm floating on air as we eat our dinner, Archie keeps complimenting me on how good it is. I think he's being polite as I'm not renowned for my culinary expertise…I'm a shit cook! We talk about out jobs, the marketing campaign for chocolate cookies I'm working on pales into insignificance compared to him saving lives in A&E. Then I start to worry, am I clever enough for him? Am I too lightweight for an A&E doctor? Do I need to be less Camilla and more Sylvia? I quickly excuse myself and pop to the loo to check my phone. I quickly search top ten intelligent conversation starters…shit this is well out of my depth but I'll give it a try. When I return to the table Archie is happily digging in to some chocolate trifle which I'm glad to say I didn't make myself;

'So Archie, what do you think is the purpose of art in society?'

He looks at me and bursts out laughing;

'To be honest Ann, I haven't got a fucking clue.'

That makes me laugh and soon we are howling with laughter together. I get up to put the dishes in the sink and I can sense Archie behind me. I turn around, he puts his arm around my waist and pulls me into him;

'I've wanted to kiss you from the first moment I saw you.'

I quickly pinch myself to make sure this is not another one of those vivid dreams I have and it's real…so what's the catch? Has he parked a swingers caravan outside? Is he really Sylvia's love child? Is he going to spill hot wax on his own bellend? I decide not to analyse the situation too much and enjoy the moment;

'What are you waiting for?'

With that he kisses me and it's possibly the best kiss I have ever had, my whole body tingles as he kisses me like he actually really means it. We head to the bedroom shedding clothes as we go, when I'm down to my basque he gently kisses my neck and slips his hand between my legs. I gasp as he kneads my clit, he definitely has healing hands! I unzip his trousers and as his cock stands erect in front of me I remember the surprise I wanted to give him.

'Just stop a minute Archie, I have a surprise for you.'

He gives me an excited smile and throws himself down on the bed. I run to the bathroom and change into a sexy nurse outfit...he's going to love this! I straighten the little hat and pump up my tits so there's an indecent amount of cleavage popping over the top of the dress. I feel like the dog's bollocks as I head back to the bedroom, I'm going to give Archie the ride of his life. I slowly open the bedroom door...I'm milking every moment of this and Archie catches sight of me. His eyes look like they are going to pop our of his head and then...he laughs a real guttural laugh that shakes his whole body. That wasn't really the reaction I was looking for and he's not stopping;

'I'm sorry Ann, you look sexy as hell. I'm a doctor and you've dressed as a nurse, you've got to see the funny side.'

I give a polite giggle as he carries on roaring with laughter. Then as suddenly as he started, he stops and clutches his chest...what the fuckity fuck. All the colour has drained from his face and he seems to be in pain...please don't tell me he's having a heart attack, I can't be that unlucky that two dates have a heart attack on me. I feel like something out of ancient history 'beware the Ann without an 'e' just one look from her and you'll have a heart attack...I'm cursed!

'Shit Archie, should I call an ambulance?'

'No, no it's fine…just a pulled muscle.'

He's a doctor so he should know if it's a pulled muscle, but I'm not taking any chances and call a taxi to take us to the hospital. I throw my coat on and help Archie sort his clothes out. He's really not happy about going to the hospital but I'm not taking no for an answer.

We arrive at A&E and Archie is still clutching his chest as we head towards the reception desk. Little Miss Smug Bitch is waiting and her eyes narrow in disgust as she sees me, but light up as she clocks Archie;

'Archie…what's happened?'

Archie begins to explain about the pain in his chest but she can't take her eyes off the top of my head, I'm starting to feel self- conscious;

'You've got something on your head.'

I haven't got a clue what she's talking about until I touch my hair and realise I'm still wearing the little nurses hat. I quickly pull it off and shove it into my pocket…for fucks sake, how did I forget to take that off, I wondered why everyone was looking at us when we walked in. Thankfully she doesn't give her usual loud run down of why I've come to A&E…she doesn't give a shit about me, she's saving the Archie the embarrassment of his sexual shenanigans being aired in public. Thankfully we don't have to wait as Little Miss Smug Bitch works her magic and gets Archie taken straight to a cubicle.

'I'm sorry about this Ann, I've ruined what was a brilliant evening, can you ever forgive me.'

He's such a sweetheart, even though he's potentially having a heart attack, he's still thinking about me;

'Of course you haven't ruined the evening, it wouldn't be me without a trip to A&E.'

He gives me a cheeky knowing smile and squeezes my hand…it's probably inappropriate to think it given the circumstances but I wish he was squeezing my fanny!

Archie has had the undivided attention of his colleagues, he's had a number of tests done and now we are just waiting for the doctor on duty to come and let us know the results. It's not long before the curtain is pulled back in one quick swish and there standing before me is my nemesis…Sylvia. She has her head down reading Archie's notes and doesn't notice me;

'I was just on my way home Archie, but I wanted to let you know everything is fine, it looks like you pulled your pectoral muscle which as you know can be very painful…you need to be more careful, what on earth were you doing?'

At which point she notices me…she gives me her famous death stare and I swear she's trembling with anger. She throws her bag down on the bed and steps towards me;

'I should have known you'd be involved…he can't resist a pretty face. You just can't leave the good ones alone can you?'

She spits the words out with real venom, she's clearly never going to forgive me for having the audacity to date her precious Josh. Archie is clearly riled by her words;

'Sylvia, I don't know what you have against Ann, but we are in a relationship and I'd ask you to respect that.'

We're in a what now? Did he really say we are in a relationship…all that stuff I said about no strings sex and relationships being shit, forget it…me and Dr Gorgeous are a thing. I'm so excited I almost miss it when Sylvia angrily pulls her bag off the bed, it's not zipped up and something falls out and lands at my feet. I bend down to pick it up for her. It takes me a few seconds to register what I have in my hands…it's a pink flamingo mask! Fucking hell…Sylvia is the flamingo! Sylvia, paragon of virtue, judgemental bitch from hell, hater of love lumps is the flamingo! I was convinced it was Camilla, never in my wildest dreams would I have imagined Sylvia was a regular on the local dogging and swinging scene. Sylvia looks crest fallen as I hand her the mask, she knows that I know and the question is, what am I going to do about it?

'Here you go Sylvia, what a pretty mask. I've heard about the lady in flamingo mask who visits the children's ward...well done you.'

Her shoulders relax as the relief I haven't exposed her secret flows through her. She mutters something under her breath shoves the mask back into her bag and leaves without a second glance. I know she's been an evil witch but I could never embarrass another woman like that. What she does with her minge is absolutely nothing to do with me. Good on her I say, she's far more sexually liberated than I could ever be...a true erotic goddess, now who would have thought that!

Archie comes back to mine and we head straight to bed...unfortunately he's still in pain so we just snuggle;

'Archie, did you mean it when you said we were in a relationship?'

'Of course I did, that's if you want to be?'

'Hmmm, let me think about it...yes please!

Who'd have though all those months ago when Dr Gorgeous was examining my muff balls that we'd end up in a relationship...this is all playing out rather well and I start to wonder what the universe is going to throw into the mix to ruin it. I suppose I just have to enjoy every moment, maybe this time my luck really has changed. I try to sleep with my head on Archies' chest…that is the romantic thing to do after all. But his abundant chest hair is tickling my nose and getting into my mouth…fuck that, I give him a quick pat and roll over onto my own side of the bed. I drift off to sleep listening to the gentle sound of his breathing and I finally feel content.

Archie left earlier this morning, he tried not to wake me as he gently kissed me goodbye…it didn't work as soon as his lips touched mine my fanny alarm clock went off and I was wide awake. He had to rush because he needed to get home and change before he started his shift. Before he left he invited me to the hospital Christmas ball…so we really are official. It's in two days so I have a lot of planning to do. My head is full of dresses, crotchless knickers and nipple clamps when my phone rings. I assume it's Archie ringing me to tell me he's missing me already so I don't look at the number. I nearly choke on my coffee when I answer and it's Sylvia;

'Hello Ann, I feel I owe you an explanation and an apology. Can you meet me at the clock tower in the park in half an hour.'

What the fuck is going on? What could she possibly have to say to me…she can't stand me, in her eyes I'm the feckless floozy that tried to seduce her little man. I'm so curious I agree to meet her. What could she possibly have to say? I quickly have a wash, brush my teeth and throw some clothes on. This is going to be interesting and I'm not sure whether or not I should be a little bit scared, this is Sylvia after all. I've put my trainers on just in case I have to make a run for it.

CHAPTER SIX

Sylvia

I'm waiting by the clock tower for Sylvia and I have butterflies in my stomach. I can't quite believe that I am willingly waiting for the mad bitch troll from hell. She did say she wanted to apologise so I don't think she's going to out me as a scarlet woman in front of the local dog walking club or threaten me with certain death if I reveal her hidden identity. She also said she wanted to explain, but explain what exactly? The suspense is killing me but thankfully I don't have too long to wait, I can see Sylvia approaching and as gets closer she actually smiles. Her eyes look softer and she's not shooting me her usual psychotic death glare. She walks up to me arms outstretched and actually gives me a hug, I don't know how to respond so stand still with my arms firmly against my side…this is not at all awkward, not at all! Sylvia gestures to a park bench and we sit down;

'Thanks for coming today Ann, I feel like I've judged you unfairly and I wanted to explain. When you found my flamingo mask you could have told everyone, you could have humiliated me and ruined my reputation but you chose not to. Even though I've been cruel to you, you still protected my secret and I can't thank you enough for that. I thought you were a heartless strumpet who was going to take advantage of my son and then cast him aside when something better came along. I misjudged you.'

I'm quite taken aback by this…she is being nice, how did that happen? What happened to the old Sylvia? I'm wondering whether the real Sylvia has been abducted by aliens and replaced by a clone and strumpet, where have I heard that before?…oh yes I remember, Josh called me a fuck strumpet. I am warming to the new Sylvia but what the hell do they talk about around the dinner table;

'I met a lovely girl last night Mum'

'Is she a strumpet'

'No Mum she's really lovely.'

' So she's a slut then?'

Having played out that scenario in my mind, I'm desperate to laugh out loud, but Sylvia carries on with her story and it's important that listen to her;

'When I was at school I wasn't one of the pretty, popular girls. I was the clever kid, the geek, the butt of all the jokes. I didn't have many friends and when the other girls started seeing boys, no boy would even give me a second glance, but I didn't care because I was focused on getting to medical school. That was all the mattered. I flew through all my exams and got into one of the best medical schools in the country. I also met my husband Steven, he was very similar to me and I'd say we were kindred spirits. I was his first and he was mine, we even waited until our wedding night until we had sex for the first time. We were married not long after we finished university and within no time I had Maria and then Josh. Maybe it's because he hadn't lived enough or maybe because we hardly had anytime alone before we had children, Steven felt trapped. He wanted to experience all the things he'd missed out on when he was studying. He became a Dad too soon and the responsibility was too much for him. He left me for a pretty young nurse and I was devastated. She was everything I wasn't, everything I could never hope to be and it left me deeply suspicious of beautiful women. I was heartbroken, my whole world had been cruelly snatched away from me but I had to carry on. I had children to bring up and a career to carve out. The moment he left I decided I would never give my heart to another man.'

Poor Sylvia I'm starting to see why she's so bitter and twisted and I can relate to her experiences at school. How ironic that years later it was her daughter bullying me for being the geeky kid. This must be so hard for her. I don't suppose she opens up to anyone, so rather than interrupt her I just nod sympathetically;

'The years passed and although I'd only ever had sex with Steven, I felt I was missing out on something and I had never been a fan of self- satisfaction. I thought about using male escorts but the thought of paying for sex troubled me. Then one evening I overheard a colleague talking about swingers…he wasn't being too complimentary but I decided to do some research and it looked like the perfect solution. I started looking into local swingers clubs and eventually found the courage to go along. It did worry me that I might be recognised so that's where the flamingo mask comes in. I chose a flamingo because they elegant, vibrant and beautiful…so as soon as I put on the mask, that's what I became. It excited me to be completely anonymous, it meant for a couple of glorious hours I could forget who I was. The first event I went to was an education, at first I felt like a spare part standing in the corner not knowing what to do, but as soon as I was asked to join in I took to it like a duck to water. It was strange at first, I'd never seen so many cocks.'

Oh my God, Sylvia just said 'cocks'…I have to stop myself sniggering.

'I felt liberated, all those suppressed feeling and desires I'd had over the years were satisfied in one night of anonymous sex. So that's where it began and now I suppose you would say I'm a regular and I'll be totally honest with you...I do enjoy it. I enjoy the thrill of getting ready to go out and I can't get enough of the sex...it is amazing! When I feel the need, I take myself off into the countryside or book myself into an event in a hotel. I'm part of a community and we keep in touch regularly to let each other know when we'll be meeting up. I love the anonymity, I'm just known as flamingo...I suppose you could say it's my alter ego. I only have to look after me own needs. I can have sex and walk away, I don't have to give a thing emotionally and I won't be let down...apart from the odd one who can't maintain an erection, I'm always very patient with them and of course recommend they go and see their GP. I've been on the scene so long now, some men specifically search out the flamingo. I suppose that must mean I'm a good shag'.

...and now she said 'shag'. I'm really struggling not laugh.

'I'm so very sorry I was so horrible to you when you came to see Josh that evening. When my husband left, I made a vow to protect my children from heartache. Maria is fine, she's as hard as nails and she has never needed me...or liked me come to think of it. I think you knew her from school, Josh said she bullied you because of your braces. Josh however is a completely different story, he is kind and gentle. He's been my little shadow from the day he was born, we did everything together and looking back I think I sheltered him too much. He has a big heart and I didn't want to see it trampled all over, when I saw you…beautiful and confident with a magnificent cleavage I automatically assumed you would hurt him…I was wrong and I'm sorry. I can see now you would have been good for Josh, he needs a good strong woman. Don't get me wrong, his new girlfriend is perfectly lovely but she's not as feisty as you. There is something about her I can't put my finger on, she reminds me of someone but I don't know who. You see, I'm doing it again aren't I? I'm getting too involved in his life, he's happy and that's all that matters…you've made me realise that Ann.'

Sylvia is being so complimentary I'm shocked, my tits have called many things but 'magnificent', I'll take that! I'm pleased she's going to take a step back from Josh's life…the poor guy has a Mummy complex and she needs to cut the cord.

'There's no need to apologise Sylvia, you were just trying to protect your child…I understand that now. You did scare the shit out of me though! When I left your house, I half expected you to run after me with a meat cleaver in your hand.'

Sylvia laughs, her whole face softens and she looks like a

different person. I've never noticed what lovely eyes she has, they are deep blue and twinkle as she laughs. I suppose that's because I've only ever seen her narrow them in disgust as she gives me one of her inimitable death stares.

'I do seem to have that effect on people, but I am actually quite nice…honestly. I just have a low tolerance for any form of silliness and I'm not particularly trusting. I've put up a brick wall over the years and you've convinced me I need to start knocking it down and start to trust again. I hope you'll be happy with Archie, you make a good couple…but don't hurt him or you'll have me to deal with. You made an impression on him from the first time he saw you…that was the time you presented with swollen labia wasn't it?'

It was all going so well until she mentioned my fanny flaps and I feel myself inwardly cringe. Oh well what's a pair of muff testicles between friends and I actually think we could be friends;

'I'm so pleased you agreed to meet me Ann. Archie told me you're coming to the Christmas ball, you must let me buy you a drink or two…it's the least I can do after everything you've done for me. You've made me take a long hard look at myself and convinced me that I do have to make some changes. Anyway I must get off. I'm due at the hospital in a couple of hours and then tonight I might just be turning into my beloved flamingo...as long as it doesn't rain, I do hate being fucked in the rain.'

Sylvia saying 'fucked' finished me off and I burst out laughing, thankfully she laughs too and hugs me again. This time I'm less shocked and reciprocate. Well, what a fucking revelation that was!   As I'm walking home I ponder what Sylvia has said. I don't know whether to feel sorry for her or admire her. Her husband leaving her obviously had a profound effect, but she took control of her own destiny and everything she does is on her own terms. When I first saw the flamingo mask, I thought she was an erotic goddess to be admired. But she's totally closed the door on any relationships because she's scared of getting hurt. Maybe there is someone out there who would make her happy...they would have to have balls of steel and an interest in al-fresco sex but there could be a Mr Romance and Mr Uninhibited waiting for someone just like her. Anyway, what do I know, she comes to life when she talks about her adventures as the flamingo. Maybe she's got the right idea...she gets shit loads of sex and never has to wash dirty socks.

Of all the strange experiences I've had over the last few months, that has to be one of the strangest. I feel uplifted as I make my way home, I came face to face with my nemesis and she was actually alright...who would have thought when

I first met Sylvia that beneath that puritanical exterior was a right goer! I do hope she softens up a bit now, there is a genuinely lovely woman under that terrifying exterior and I'm sure Josh would appreciate a break from her obsessive interest in his love life. So now I can tick 'make my peace with Sylvia' off my to do list, I have to make plans for the Christmas Ball…what am I going to wear? Hair up or down? Do I need another spray tan? Am I going to get a shag?

CHAPTER SEVEN

Archie - again

Tonight's the night of the ball and I'm beyond excited. I had my hair done this morning, I've had it coloured…getting too many bastard grey hairs to just keep pulling them out and it's been straightened to within an inch of its life. I was also horrified to discover it's not just the hair on my head that's turning grey. I found a grey hair growing in my lady garden…it was too late to consider a muff dye (do they even exist?) so I had to pluck…fuck me it hurt! Thankfully my eyebrows are grey free, I had them threaded so they are beautifully arched and there's not a hint of a mono-brow. I was slightly offended when the technician asked me if she wanted to do my top lip and chin whilst she was at it…what the fuck was she trying to say? As for another spray tan, I decided against it…I want to look radiant and that doesn't mean glowing like a Belisha beacon. I'm wearing a long black dress and as Sylvia said, my cleavage looks magnificent…if Archie doesn't want to rub his face in these bad boys I may as well give up. I'm wearing heels, but not too high…I've learnt my lesson when it comes to high shoes…they just don't work for me! So that's me, ready for my big night out with Dr Gorgeous, I've just got time for a glass of Prosecco and a quick cigarette before Archie arrives…he must never know that I smoke, he's bound to disapprove.

I've just about finished my cigarette when the door bell rings…shit he's early. I down my drink and hunt for a mint, I can't go outside smelling like an ashtray. I'm flapping around like a pissed off chicken trying to get rid of the smoke. When I'm convinced it's gone I give myself a couple of squirts of perfume, thankfully find a packet of mints in the drawer and answer the door. Archie looks fanny tinglingly gorgeous…he kisses me on the lips and I push the mint I'm sucking on to the front of my mouth in the hope he tastes mint rather than tobacco;

'Hi Ann, you look absolutely stunning…can you smell smoke?'

'Thanks Archie…no, not really. It might be coming from the guy next door…he smokes like a chimney, it's a terrible habit.'

We get into the taxi and I feel a little bad blaming my neighbour but a girl's got to do what a girl's got to do and all that. I don't want to put Archie off so early on in our relationship. He holds my hand for the entire journey and I feel so happy…tonight is going to be a good night and I get the feeling I'm going to have a very happy fanny by the end of it.

We arrive at the venue and walk in together hand in hand…we really are a proper couple and I still can't quite believe my luck. The room is beautiful, it's been transformed into a winter wonderland complete with fake snow, icicles and Christmas trees. It's really romantic…yes I'm allowing a bit of romance in my life. Let's face it, I probably was never cut out to be an erotic goddess and chatting to Sylvia has made me realise if I don't take a chance on romance I might end up too scared of rejection to even try. Talk of the devil…Sylvia is at the bar and looks absolutely delighted to see me;

'Ann, over here…let me get you that drink.'

Sylvia hands me a glass of Prosecco and as her and Archie chat I feel a tap on my shoulder, I turn round and to my surprise it's Josh;

'Hi Ann, it's great to see you again. I just wanted to thank you, I don't know what you said to my Mum, but she's like a different woman…she's almost normal. It's good to see you happy, Archie is a great guy…he's a lucky guy.'

That was very sweet of him but before I can respond his girlfriend spots us talking and drags him off demanding to know who the fuck I was…I think the words she used were 'who the fuck is that slut?' I thought Sylvia said she wasn't feisty? Poor Josh, well at least Sylvia is leaving him alone now…but I think he may have found himself the mirror image of his Mother. Sylvia clearly hasn't seen it yet, but the person Josh's girlfriend reminds her of, is herself. I put my arm around Archie's waist and he kisses me…I feel like dragging him to the nearest toilet and fucking him, but this is his works Christmas do and I have to make a good impression on his colleagues. This evening is definitely going to be a battle of mind over fanny…mind says be sensible…fanny says come and get it! Archie is introducing me to so many of his colleagues. They are all very sweet and I've got three gasses of Prosecco lined up on the bar…they keep buying me drinks and I feel awful because I'm not sure I'm going to remember all their names;

'Ann, this is Stacey.'

I recoil in horror as I recognise her straight away…it's Little Miss Smug Bitch from reception. She looks completely different…more relaxed and much more friendly. I smile and inwardly cringe as I wait for her to say something humiliating ;

'Hi again Ann.'

Oh shit here it comes…

'It's so good to meet you properly. You've only ever seen

my work persona before…I don't know what it is, but as soon as I get behind that reception desk I take on a different identity. I become somewhat dictatorial and I'm so sorry I was so loud. When you came in, I couldn't believe what I was hearing and by repeating it I knew I'd heard right. It must have been a bit embarrassing for you though, especially the hair remover cream and oh my God the love balls…I haven't laughed so much as the day you walked in chiming away like the town hall clock on New Years Eve. Every time you come in you give us a laugh, you could write a book about your adventures or should I call them mis-adventures? You must let me buy you a drink.'

Mis-adventures? No, lets just call them fuck ups and be done with it. It's good to know I've kept the A&E department laughing over the past few months…if I end up in the Daily Mail, I know who to blame. Stacey hands me a Prosecco and I more or less down it in one…I needed too as everyone in my immediate vicinity now knows about my fanny fails. My confidence restored I drag Archie onto the dance floor…he's quite a mover and we are just as we are about to start smooching to a slow number, Sylvia grabs my hand…for fuck's sake she doesn't half choose her moments;

'Ann, my special friend the flamingo wants to buy you a drink.'

I think she's pissed and I'm not far behind her. She gets me another Prosecco from the bar and then hands me a shot of Sambuca;

'Come on Ann, down it I one…down it, down it, down it!'

What the fuck is going on? Sylvia has completely let her hair down, it's like she's making up for all those lost years. She's a doctor, should she really be encouraging me to drink? Fuck it, I down the Sambuca in one and gasp as the heat hits my chest…I like the new Sylvia, I like her a lot! In the time it took me to drink the Sambuca, Sylvia has disappeared…I ask Archie where she's gone and he gestures to a crowd on the dance floor. Curious, I make my way through a sea of bodies and there in the centre of the circle is Sylvia, complete with flamingo mask performing a rather enthusiastic dance routine to I will survive by Gloria Gaynor. I watch in awe as she gyrates around the circle interacting with the bemused onlookers. She seems to be singling out one particular man in the crowd and his discomfort is palpable…does she fancy him or has he been treated to the full flamingo performance before? Has the poor man just been hit by the realisation that the best shag on the local dogging circuit is actually his boss? Before Sylvia can launch into a final chorus of the song Josh appears and tries to remove her from the circle…

'Come on Mum, I think it's time to go home.'

To Josh's horror and my absolute delight, Sylvia tells him to fuck off and carries on dancing. He looks crest fallen and his girlfriend is furious. I leave Sylvia to her audience and go to find Archie, I feel like I've hardly seen him this evening. He's chatting to a short, chubby man who has the most amazing comb over…

'Ann, I'd like you to be Robert…he's one of the hospital's biggest charitable donors.'

Robert is dripping in chunky gold jewellery and his clothes although straining to fit in certain places are clearly high end designer. I try not to stare at his hair as he shakes my hand vigorously and immediately starts to talk to me like we are old friends. I warm to him straight away, he's a jolly man with a ruddy cheeks and a booming laugh. He calls a spade a spade and he's absolutely hilarious…I wonder if I could fix him up with Sylvia? He hands me a glass of Prosecco and just as I'm about to enquire about his romantic status he starts waving at someone…

'Here's my girlfriend, she's just been to wet the lettuce.'

Oh my God, 'wet the lettuce'…Robert is a scream! I'm wondering what his girlfriend is going to be like, I hope he's just like him. Unfortunately my hope is short lived…

'Guys, this is Camilla.'

I shit you not…Camilla as in Daniel, Camilla as in Ryan. She may not have been the flamingo, but she's clearly fucking stalking me. I see a flicker of recognition in her eyes as she strokes her hair protectively…she knows exactly who I am. As Robert chats to Archie, I manage to take her to one side;

'So what the fuck happened to Ryan?'

'Who? Oh yes, him. Well his silly little paintings were doing very well in the gallery and he became Daddy's new pet. All he ever talked about was paint and chalk. Quite frankly I found it boring. He wasn't paying me any attention so I finished with him. Then I met Bobby. Bobby treats me like a princess, he'll do anything for me. He's taking me to St Lucia for Christmas and buying me a whole new wardrobe for the trip.'

So basically she's going to bleed Robert dry and then move on to the next poor bastard…why did I ever think being like her was a good idea. She cares about no one except herself. I don't think she ever wanted Ryan. She liked him, found out he was with someone and then made it her mission to take him for herself…what a fucking bitch! I feel like telling Robert exactly what she's like, but he seems happy. She's putting a spring in his step, making him feel young. I take satisfaction from the look of disgust on

Camilla's face as Robert squeezes her arse and tells her he can't wait to get her home. The party is starting to wind up as we chat to Robert and I'm feeling pretty shit faced…how much prosecco have I had? I'm pleased we are leaving, Camilla was starting to give Archie the eye and I'm not losing this one to Miss Fucking Perfection Personified. We head outside to get a taxi and as soon as the fresh air hits me I forget how to use my legs and I start to stumble incoherently…I need to sober up, I've got unfinished business with Archie's cock.

We get back to Archie's and I make myself at home in the living room whilst Archie makes me a cup of coffee…he seems a bit worried, maybe it was because I fell over when we got out of the taxi. I blame my shoes…you know what I'm like with shoes. Or was it because I kept telling him how much I liked him…maybe I shouldn't have told the taxi driver my fanny was tingling. His sitting room is homely and comfortable, so comfortable I could quite easily fall asleep I decide I need to keep myself awake and give Archie a surprise when he gets back from the kitchen. I take off me dress and adopt my best 'come and get me big boy' pose on the sofa. Archie walks back in and nearly drops my coffee;

'Ann! Are you ok, did you fall over again?'

No Archie, I didn't fall over I'm trying to look sexy. I

think the fact I'm dribbling a bit might have taken away from the moment. I must admit, I don't feel altogether well and before I can say 'Where's the bathroom I'm going to be sick', I vomit all over Archie's shoes. Archie manages to get me to the bathroom and holds my hair whilst I'm sick again and again. He rubs my back and talks to me gently…I feel like a complete twat and start ugly drunk crying. I'm convinced I've blown it, how could he possibly like me when I've just vomited on his shoes. I've probably ruined them and I don't think the rug in his sitting room will ever be the same again. In between heaves, I promise to pay for any dry cleaning. He's so lovely and tells me I don't need to think about paying for anything. When he's convinced I'm finished he helps me wash and takes me to the bedroom. He gives me one of his shirts and I start to cry again;

'I'm so sorry Archie…I wanted tonight to be special.'

'It has been special Ann and we've got plenty more nights to come.'

Archie leaves me to go and clean the sitting room…he's perfect isn't he? I fall asleep pissed but happy, I haven't fucked it up and Archie wants to spend more time with me…I think this time I might have actually done it. I've definitely found my Mr Romance and I have no doubt he's going to be my Mr Uninhibited.

CHAPTER EIGHT

Lessons Learnt

It's Christmas day and I'm spending it with…Archie!!! My Mum was pissed off at first, but as soon as I told her Archie was a doctor she suddenly changed her tune;

'Of course you must spend the day with Archie…ohhh we've never had a doctor in the family. I must phone your Aunty Jean and tell her…she'll be so jealous. So I'll be meeting him on Boxing Day will I? I'll tell your Dad to get a bottle of that nice whiskey in.'

My Mum comes from that generation where doctors are thought of as super human…I've earnt a shit load of daughter brownie points and she's going to roll out the red carpet for him when she gets to meet him on Boxing Day. I wouldn't be surprised if she does a curtsey on the door step when she sees him. I just hope and pray, she doesn't invite the entire family round to meet him, it's the sort of thing she would do to claim bragging rights. Anyway enough of my Mother and back to Archie. I had a hangover for two days after the Christmas do. Archie was really sweet and kept popping to mine to check on me. On the second day when I was feeling better he came over in the evening and I'm pleased to report I fucked him…I fucked him in the kitchen, in the bedroom, in the shower and in the garden shed (he caught me having a crafty cigarette and well, one thing led to another). I think we tried every position known to man and God could he keep going…Archie is definitely not a two minute wonder. When it was time for him to leave, I waved him goodbye from my bed…not because I was tired, but because I couldn't fucking walk! It was everything I imagined sex should be and he absolutely made sure all my needs were met. So here we are together at Christmas, he's in the kitchen basting the turkey…he'll be basting me later, but I want to open my presents first. I've finally found my Mr Romance and my Mr Uninhibited…I can't even begin to tell you what he got up to with my Ann Summers stash! It's taken me quite some time and I've learnt even more over the last few months.

The first lesson I learnt was never trust an artist (that may be a generalisation but I'm allowed to be bitter and twisted). Ryan built up my trust and destroyed it in an instant. He was all ethereal and arty…you can trust me because I have a soul. Utter bollocks he was driven by his cock like every other man (obviously not including Archie). He was selfish in the bedroom, driven by his own needs…that should have been a clue that the most important person in Ryan's life was Ryan. For all his talk of love and a future he soon dropped me when he met Camilla. Now that was double whammy not only was she Miss Fucking Perfection Personified but her Dad held the key to Ryan's art career...I was never going to win that battle. Losing Ryan made me feel like I should be more like Camilla, but that was wrong. Why would I want to be like a woman who deliberately uses her feminine wiles to hurt other women. Why should I change my appearance just to attract men...no I am what I am and you can like it or fuck off. I can't even get a spray tan without it going wrong, so any form of plastic surgery is completely off the table. I was never going to be an erotic goddess, but that doesn't mean I can't be a great shag.

When online dating, make sure your know your terminology. I am of course referring to water sports...how was I supposed to know he was referring to the art of peeing on each other. I really should have checked on line before I agreed to it. I didn't even know that was a thing and now I have a wet suit hanging in my wardrobe that I'm never going to use, can you seriously imagine me water skiing or surfing...no, neither can I. Which brings me on to Leo. What can say? Firstly seagulls are cunts and will stop at nothing to get their greedy beaks on your delicious sugary donuts...they really have no fear and let nothing stand between them and food... a bit like Camilla and men.

Secondly, if your date asks you to go to the beach in the middle of winter be suspicious if they ask you to take your shoes off. What was I thinking exposing my toes to the elements? Why did I not cotton on when he asked me to describe what the sand felt like between my toes or when he started to take photographs of my feet? You need a man to be interested in you, the whole package…it doesn't matter if you have lovely feet. It's you as a person that matters. He was such a good looking guy with a lovely personality…if he could just extend his desire for women beyond the ankle he would be fighting them off. Leo still messages me every so often to ask if I'll send him pictures of my feet in various poses…maybe I'll send him a picture of Archies feet and see what he thinks of them!

Never ever agree to wear a green scarf on a blind date…they are fucking hard to get hold of and look far too much like old school scarves for my liking. Which brings me onto Joe, he was an actual man mountain of Adonis like proportions…he was absolutely gorgeous, witty, intelligent but far too sensitive. In Joe's world, sneezing, burping and farting just did not exist…but sneezing, burping and farting are all part of life's rich tapestry, they come with the territory. Ok, I did actually fart just as he as about to go down on me. But looking back on it, it was actually quite funny and something we could have told the Grandchildren about. It could have been worse, it could have been a flap slapper...how would he have coped with that? You have to be prepared to accept your partner farts and all...if he doesn't make some changes quickly Joe is going to have to go and live on a desert island. I still can't get my head around it, how does he cope with his own bodily functions? Does he give himself a bollocking and run out of the room every time he farts or is it just other peoples farts he doesn't like? My friend Veronica found it hilarious when I told her. She bought a fart machine which she hid in her desk drawer and set off every time Joe walked passed. It's wicked but maybe it will be a form of therapy for him!

Don't be charmed by a cheeky chappie. Luke was hilarious with a cheeky glint in his eye. He charmed me over coffee with a view to sharing me with his swinging mates. Or it could just have been I was giving out swinging vibes...I was quite flirtatious and looking back might have intimated I was up for anything...but come on, he shouldn't have made the assumption. Don't be oblivious to the clues staring you in the face...hotel in the middle of nowhere, boxes of tissues everywhere, condoms in the bedroom, random couples trying to make conversation, couples mixing and matching in the hot tub. No wonder he was so excited when I agreed you could fit six people in the bedroom, he was gearing up for us having a full on orgy. Why did it take me until I saw the human centipede in the hot tub to realise what the fuck was going on? Luke had no right putting me in that situation without warning me…never do anything you don't want to, if it makes you uncomfortable then don't do it. I may have wanted to be a sexually liberated erotic goddess but that doesn't include sharing my fanny to all and sundry. I know it's quite popular and each to their own but I'm not out to emulate Sylvia just yet!

Which brings me to Sylvia…what the fuck! I was seriously convinced that the flamingo was Camilla…after all she did seem to be following me around. Never in a million years would I ever have thought it was Sylvia. I have to admit when I first saw the flamingo mask fall out of her bag, I did for a split second feel like telling the world, but I saw something in her eyes that made me stop. I'm so pleased I didn't betray her secret. She holds so much sorrow, imagine being let down so badly by the love of your life that you vow never to have a relationship again. Sylvia devoted her life to her children and her career. The flamingo provided her with a release and allowed her to fulfil her sexual desires, she lives the life she didn't have through that mask and no one can judge her for it. I just hope that she really does start to lighten up now…I bet she had a really bad hangover after the Christmas party. She really was the life and soul of the party and I'm sure it was a revelation to her colleagues… she's got years of partying to catch up on and she made a great start. I wonder what she was like on her first morning back at work, did she walk into the A&E department high fiving everyone on the way in or did she shoot them her death stare defying anyone to mention the events of the night before. There will be someone out there for Sylvia and now I'm going to be seeing a lot more of her, I'm going to make it my mission to find him. It's strange how things turn out, I hated Sylvia with a passion…she had treated me with such contempt and I saw bits of her in every horror film I had ever watched and now…she's my bestie!

Finally, never give up hope. After all my relationship and dating disasters I was toying with the idea of doing a Sylvia. I thought it would easier to detach myself and just use men for sex…I didn't get very far with that did I? Just as I was about to give up along came Archie, my very own Dr Gorgeous. From that first time he looked at my muff testicles, I knew there was something special about him…it's like it was written in the stars and we were destined to be together. I should never have held Camilla up as some sort of role model. Miss Fucking Perfection Personified…but was she? She judges men on what they can do for her and changes them as often as she changes her knickers…I hope she'll be happy with Robert but I'm sure she'll dump him when she's had her holiday and new wardrobe to go with it. The look on her face when he was slobbering all over her was priceless…serves her fucking right! It's not been long, but I think I can safely say Archie is 'the one'. He's the Mr Romance and Mr Uninhibited I've been searching for…I know now it was never meant to be Daniel or Tom or Ryan. It was always going to be Archie and I'm so happy I'm crying happy tears.

Hold on my phone has just pinged with a message… it's a festive dick pic and either he's really into Christmas or he's had too much of the Christmas spirit as he's put a little Santa hat on the end of it. I wish the mystery schlong a happy Christmas and delete the dating app from my phone. I'm never going to need it again and I swear, if it doesn't work out with Archie I am definitely joining a nunnery. At least now I can look back at the burnt bellend, BDSM disaster, mad Mother, defective handcuffs, anaconda dick, dogging, the Hershey Highway, O.A. Pervert, stupidly high shoes, swinging, over sensitivity and farting at an inopportune moment and laugh! I may have been shit at dating but I got what I wanted in the end. I'm having the best Christmas I could possibly have wished for and as soon as I've unwrapped the presents in my stocking I'm going to unwrap the best present of all…Dr Gorgeous.

'

Thank you for reading my book, I hope you enjoyed it! If you did could you please take the time to leave a positive review for it. I have you have any questions or suggestions then I always welcome them and you can email me directly at reallyreallynovel@gmail.com

And...while I still I have you here I'd like to recommend a book of short stories from my talented brother, Richard Hennerley. The book is called 'I Really, Really Want It' and it's an outrageous thriller set in the world of celebrity that is by turns very funny, shockingly outrageous and very, very dark...here's the book blurb and some sample chapters...

I Really Really Want It

Fame. Lies. Scandal. Drugs. Sex. *MURDER*. Celebrities have secrets to die for.

Andrew Manning has spent 20 years saving celebrities from the consequences of their own bad behavior and is known in the business as' The King of Scandal'. But now some particularly difficult and demanding characters are about strain even his legendary abilities:

Shelley, model and fashion icon, who's determined not just to blackmail her equally famous husband but also to destroy him.

Joey, an insecure reality TV star, desperate to hang on to his celebrity, even if it means slowly poisoning himself to death.

The Producer, a king in the world of entertainment and a serial abuser of hopeful young wannabe's. But this time he's picked the wrong girl for his perverted pleasures.

Charlie, morbidly obese, murderous mafiosi adviser to...

Janey, pop music goddess, a celebrity with peculiarly sharp teeth and disturbing eating habits that are about to be revealed to the public by an ambitious young paparazzo.

And then there's Johnny, Andrew's partner, a psychopath with a heart of gold who's on a mission to murder as many celebrities as possible.

Will Andrew be able to reconcile the demands of so many different and desperate characters, and who's going to end up dead?

'I Really Really Want It', four sample chapters

Please find to follow four sample chapters (taken, more or less, from the beginning and middle of the story) from 'I Really Really Want It'.

In this first extract we meet Janey, international superstar; mad, bad, dangerous to know and possibly a vampire…

JANEY. MAKING AN ENTRANCE

As the limo speeds away from Heathrow, Janey is delighted with the way things went. What an entrance! The moment she stepped into the arrivals lounge it had been total chaos: screaming fans, paparazzi, cameramen, microphones, journalists, police, security. All there for her, Janey Jax. She is a *star*. No one comes close to her. Rivals come, rivals go and still she stays at the top, numero uno. Untouchable. Look at that Missy Go Go. Where is she now? Nowhere. Skank.

Of course, she could have flown over in the private jet, but with a world tour about to kick off and a new album coming up she needed an entrance with maximum impact, at least that's what Charlie had advised and, as always, Charlie had been right.

The day's events have left her tired, though. So tired. People forget that she's not a young girl anymore. She may still look like she's in her twenties but, in reality, she's far removed from that happy decade. Nowadays, it takes hard work to keep looking as good as she does. Hard work and fresh, young flesh. Very young flesh. She hopes Charlie won't have any problems sourcing what she needs here in England. But, no, she shouldn't worry, Charlie is very capable. He knows what she wants, and he is bound to her. By blood. He is her creature.

In this second extract we meet foul-mouthed, homophobic Shelley. Shelley wants Andrew to blackmail her famous, gay husband into giving her a huge divorce settlement, but Shelley has her own dark secret…

SHELLEY. TIME FOR A QUICK SMOKE?

Finally, the slow and tedious drive through London's crawling traffic is over and Shelley arrives at Anthea's house in Holland Park, she always stays there when she's in London. She and Anthea are Best Friends Forever. They've known each other since way back, from when they were in "Girls Gone Wild." There were four girls in the (quite successful at the time) band but Shelley only ever really liked Anthea. Chardonnay and Alicia were bitches and cunts, and where they fuck are they now? Losers! They hadn't been smart, but Anthea and Shelley had been. Shelley had used the band as a base from which to start her solo career, Anthea had exploited her celebrity and good looks to grab herself an extremely ugly but ridiculously rich banker. Christ, Shelley can feel nothing but admiration for the way she played that prick! Led him by the fucking nose, married him, stuck with him for a couple of years, then divorced him, taking almost everything he had. Honestly, men can be such gullible dickheads, show them a bit of tit and a glimpse of snatch and, in no time at all, you can have them behaving like well-trained dogs!

Once inside Anthea's house (she has her own key, that's how BFF she and Anthea are), she makes straight for the beautiful living room and throws herself into a gorgeous sofa, dropping her Prada bag onto a gorgeous coffee table, which rests on a gorgeous carpet. Shelley *really* likes Anthea's place, she makes her mind up that she too will buy a home in Holland Park when the divorce money comes through from Jack faggotpants.

Yes, the divorce settlement, more money, more success…what a wonderful day it's been! It's going to be so great when Anthea gets back from her latest shopping trip. Shelley can't wait to tell her what's about to happen to Jack, how she's about to blackmail him into a *huge* pay out. Hah, she is *so* going to screw him! Nobody fucks with Shelley!

Shelley muses happily for some minutes about her upcoming freedom from Jack and her fabulous future career in America, until her thoughts stray, unstoppably, to that package, nestled comfortably in the Prada bag. She takes it out, rolls it around in her hands, a greedy and needing expression on her face. Using her sharp finger nails, she quickly tears at and then unwraps the cellophane from the package, to reveal a substantial, round rock of crack cocaine.

She places the rock of crack on Anthea's gorgeous coffee table. Taking a nail file from her handbag she begins to chip away at the off-white coloured lump, which has a texture somewhere between wax and brittle plastic. Expertly she detaches smaller rocks from the main block, each new rock just the right size for a single good hit when smoked. There's loads of crack here, enough to last her and Anthea a couple of nights, if they don't go too mad! As well as BFFs, she and Anthea are also BDBs, Best Drug Buddies.

She loves her crack does Shelley, fantastic stuff. Okay, so maybe the next day you might feel a bit down, a bit paranoid, but nothing that can't be smoothed out with a few drinks. Or some more crack. And the hit, Christ the hit! Once felt never forgotten! She knows of course that she shouldn't really be smoking it, what with her being famous, rich and beautiful and in a responsible position due to her influence over the young people of the world, but the public just doesn't realise that being famous, rich and beautiful is very hard work. Every day is filled with questions. What should I wear? Am I slim enough? How's my make-up today? Have I got the right handbag for this or that occasion? Who should I be *seen* to be speaking to? Which party do I go to, and which should I snub? Where should I be this afternoon to stand the best chance of being papped? These are all difficult and complex questions. Being a celeb is a demanding business, not everybody can handle it. Her lifestyle involves a lot of a pressure, and the crack is Shelley's way of relaxing, of dealing with the stress she endures every day. She deserves it. She is e*ntitled* to it.

Of course she has been in trouble with the crack before, resulting in some fairly unpleasant media coverage, but she had dealt with that, although it did involve some help from that hideous queer, Andrew. But that's all in the past. She's much more careful now, more discreet, she'll never be caught again. "Never say never," says a little voice somewhere in the back of Shelley's head, but she chooses to ignore it.

Shelley wonders if she should smoke a quick rock before Anthea gets back? Why the hell not!

In this third extract we meet Joey, a handsome young reality TV star. Joey's career has gone into freefall after launching an expletive laden attack against the Queen of England on live TV. In an effort to save Joey's career, Andrew prescribes a convenient case of pretend 'celebrity cancer' but Joey has a plan of his own…

JOEY. "I LOVE THE VERY BONES OF YOU"

Joey is woken early that morning by the Philipina nurse, fussing around. Making sure all his wires and tubes are in the proper place, he presumes. Actually, is "woken" the right word? Does he really fall asleep and wake up nowadays, or does he just drift in and out of consciousness? Joey's not sure but he thinks probably the latter.

Yesterday was a big day for Joey, he's surprised that he got through it. Saying goodbye to his kids, Christ that was hard. He'd had pretty much a repeat conversation with his ma and da later on. He told them that he felt that he didn't have long left (a message that Joey knew Andy's dodgy doctor would reinforce to them). His mum kept saying "don't be silly, Joey lad, you'll get through this," but he could see from her eyes that she didn't believe it, and she could see from his that he didn't believe it either.

As he explained his (recently made up) philosophy of time as great circle, with spirits racing around it and meeting again and again as different people, but always instinctively recognising each other, well, he could see it seemed odd to his parents. At times they looked at him as though he was delirious, but he got over his central message to them. Then he explained that the twins would be their responsibility, that there was plenty of money coming their way after he died and, most of all, that he loved them dearly and he was grateful beyond words for everything they had ever done for him, that he was immensely proud that they were his parents. He wonders what they'd think should they ever find out the reason for his illness, not cancer, but his own self-administered poison. They must never know that. Joey is grateful that only Andy knows the full story behind his condition. His secrets are safe with Andy.

Having checked all his various tubes and wires, the nurse helps Joey, on his request, to move position in his bed, from lain flat to sitting up. Joey has very little strength and the poor girl has to push and pull mostly on her own. Joey's grateful that, though only a small woman, she seems to have surprising strength. Together, they get him into a sitting up in bed position. The nurse plumps up pillows behind his back, puts one behind his head. She asks him if he needs anything else, does he need the bedpan? No thanks (there's nothing in him to shit out), but could she open the curtains and maybe get him a small glass of water? Thank you.

The nurse opens the curtains, and daylight streams in. Joey thinks it must be a beautiful day outside. The realisation hits him like a physical blow. Shit. This is it. It's a beautiful day and it's this day that I'll leave this world. Today is the day I die. I'll not see any more beautiful days. I'll not see any more days, full stop. Joey is hit with a huge sense of loss. You know what, despite all the shit, all the grief and all the idiots and haters it really is a beautiful, beautiful world. His thoughts are interrupted as the nurse returns with his water. She holds the glass to his lips and helps him take a few small sips. He asks her to leave the glass by his bed.

Joey slips back into sleep/unconsciousness, he dreams. He dreams a gorgeous dream. If his dream were a film it would be in widescreen, Technicolor, 3D, high definition, the whole shooting match. He dreams he is with the twins, his ma and da are there, and Andy and three of his oldest friends from his Doncaster days: Liz, Helen and Susan. They're all at Blackpool Pleasure Beach. There's nobody else there, it's empty, fantastic, the whole thing open just for them! And Joey's body is well again, it's young, healthy, vital, it is whole.

In the dream everybody is having a great time, they eat candyfloss and donuts, the twins go mad in the arcades, piling a stream of coins, that just keep spewing from the machines like magic, into the slotties and video games. Then they hit the rides. There are no queues, nothing to pay, they just walk on. They do the Dodgems, laughing hysterically as they bump into each other, they enjoy twirling on the Teacups ride, whizzing through the air in the old Hiram Maxim flying machines, thrilled as they take a ride through time in the River Caves, pretend to get scared on the ghost train. Then after more donuts and candyfloss it's time for the grand finale: the Big Dipper. They all squeeze close up together in one giant dream-sized Big Dipper car and they're off, racing along the track. Normally Joey hates this kind of thing, but this dream Big Dipper is special. It's fast but smooth and, surrounded by such happy friends and family, Joey feels totally safe and secure. The Dipper speeds along, slows as it whizzes round a sharp bend, and then begins to climb a hill that seems to go on forever. It soars high up above the Pleasure Beach, then up above Blackpool, and looking to his left and right Joey can see way beyond the town and far out to sea. All the other rides become small, toy town in size and now the hill is so high that the view is like that from a plane. Joey is aware that the Dipper is pushing up higher and higher into the sky and he looks down and beneath him he can see big, fluffy pink clouds, like the candyfloss he has just eaten. Then huge objects appear above Joey's head: vast, snowflake-like constructions made of sparkling, clear ice, desperately beautiful and delicate and filled with a brilliant and warming, white inner light and Joey knows that they are stars. He is amazed, fascinated. They are so beautiful that they move him almost to tears. Then, as if it had decided it could go no further up, the Big Dipper car begins to descend, travelling down a huge and straight slope that seems to go on and on and on. It charges down, faster and faster, the wind whistles through Joey's hair, he feels an exhilarating freedom, everyone is loving it, Joey is loving it. But then he feels himself detach from the car, sucked out by the wind caused by its downward plunge. He's not scared, though, not worried. This sudden detachment seems like the most natural thing in the world. He flaps his arms and, just he as knew would happen, he can fly. He flies after the Dipper car for a while, but he can't keep up with its breakneck speed and he sees his family and friends are waving back at him from the car and shouting. They are smiling, they are saying "goodbye, Joey, we love you." Joey calls after them "I love you too," and stops trying to follow. He knows where he must go now, and feeling light and happy he begins to fly upward, back up to those beautiful, snowflake shaped stars.

Suddenly, Joey's dream vanishes. He is awake, disturbed by some bizarre burning pain in his chest. He's pissed off, that was a lovely dream. If only he could have stayed there! The ever present nurse has seen him stirring and ask if he's alright, "I'm fine, love," he says but grimaces in pain, the nurse notices and asks if he would like morphine. He thinks about accepting, but this is his last day, he doesn't want to spend any more of it asleep or in that warm morphine haze, so he answers in the negative and asks the nurse if she has the time and she replies, "it's just gone three o'clock , sir"

"Please, don't call me "sir" anymore, it's Joey, and you, what's your name?"

"Amor, sir...Joey."

"Amor, that's a lovely name. Amor, I want to thank you for all the 'elp you've given me, you're a great nurse an' you 'ave a very sweet nature"

Amor beams from ear to ear and says "thank you, Joey, you're a kind man, a good man."

"Now then, enough of all this compliment swapping," says Joey trying to set a light tone, "'elp me sit back up will you?"

After some mutual huffing, puffing, pulling and pushing,

Joey is back in a more upright position. Shit, he thinks, Andy will be here anytime now. He checks the glass of water is still

by his bed. Yes, it is, good. So this it. The end. He has less than an hour to live. God! He's not scared though, that dream he had has been strangely reassuring. He's ready to go, happy to go, to be honest, glad to escape the pain and discomfit that's been the main feature of his life for so long now. Sorry to leave everyone, of course, but, following his new philosophy of life and death, hopeful that it won't be for ever. Joey is about as prepared to die as any man can be.

There's a quiet knock at his bedroom door. Slowly it opens and first one head pops round, then another and another. Amazing! It's just like his bloody dream! It's Liz, Helen and Sue. "My girls!" cries Joey in delight, "come in, come in, it's so good to see you!"

The girls move as one, they come to Joey in his bed, Liz sits one side, Helen and Sue sit on the other. They're all touches and greetings, kissing Joey's cheeks, holding his hands, running their hands through his once thick hair. "Your mam called us last night, Joey," says Sue, "she told us you'd love to see us and so here we are."

"You mean," says Joey "that she told you you'd best get

down 'ere quick like, before I go."

"Well, she said you weren't good, but you're going to pull through this, Joey," says Liz.

"Liz, girls, its good of you to say that but truth is I'm dyin', but I'm ready, I don't want no tears or sympathy so you three pull ya selves together...anyway, tell me, you musta left Doncaster bloody early to get 'ere for now, how's things up there, then?"

And so it goes, Joey spends a delightful forty minutes chatting away to his three old friends. He's always loved these girls, they were his best friends at school (he never really got on with other boys, he can see now that that wasn't a failing on his part, he just pissed them off because he was too bloody good-looking). They remained friends after school, and when Joey became famous, they were always there for him, a shoulder to cry on when things were bad, a source of mostly good advice and someone to share his success with. They were never envious of that success, never asked for more than he could give, they were always true friends.

And then, sadly, this sweet little chat has to end, Andy has arrived. He's standing in the open door of Joey's bed room, looks very smart, thinks Joey. He likes Andy's suit, Armani he guesses. Joey waves Andy forward, saying, "Andy, come in, these are friends of mine from Doncaster, Liz, Helen and Sue, girls, this is Andy. 'e's a friend an' 'e kinda 'elps me out wi' me, er, legal stuff." Andy and the girls exchange handshakes and greetings, Joey can tell that Andy's a bit stressed and seems a bit hurried, he's moving a bit funny too, like somebody had kicked him in the balls. Joey senses Andy needs his attention so he says, "girls, Amor, can me an' Andy 'ave bit of privacy for a few minutes? There's some stuff I'ave to talk about wi' 'im, business, that sorta nonsense." Of course, nod the girls and the nurse and they make their way out of his room, Andy following and closing the door behind them.

"Joey," says Andy looking nervous, rubbing his hands together and smiling rather fixedly as he does so, "how are you and are you ready for this? Christ, sorry, that's a stupid question, I…I just don't really know what to say, I've never helped anyone top themselves before!"

"That's okay, Andy, it's fine, don't worry, I ain't never topped meself before so I don't know what to say either!"

"And you're sure that this is what you want, that this is what you really, really want?"

"Absolutely sure, I'm exhausted, I just can't fight to keep

meself alive anymore…just one thing, though...it won't 'urt will it, Andy…?"

In this fourth extract we meet Carrie. Carrie works for Andrew but harbours her own secret desire for celebrity. We join Carrie after she's had a bruising encounter with the sexually abusive entertainment mogul, The Producer. Ashamed and angry with herself for being so naïve, Carrie wonders what on earth she should do...until she encounters an Angel in a coffee-shop who has some good advice for her...

CARRIE'S STORY

After running out of *that* man's office, Carrie fled deeper into the anonymity of Soho, seeking shelter and safety in aloneness. She sits now in one of those soulless chain coffee shops, on her own, seat by the window, hunched over a large mug of the brown, bland muck that passes for coffee in these places, steaming like a warm cup of piss on the table in front of her.

She is appalled with herself. She is jittery. She is shaking with shame and anger. How could she have been so utterly stupid as to have her own secret dreams of stardom when she works in the world of celebrity? She knows, better than most, that it is a world of fakes and freaks, trickery, lies, abusers and cheats. But no, despite that fact, despite the fact that she's got a great, well-paid, interesting job and has lovely workmates, despite all that she has her secret, stupid bloody dream of being a singer.

And because of that, she ends up in that office. With that man. That pig. Dirty, disgusting, pig. Invited in to "discuss her career." For goodness sake, how stupidly naïve. She should have known something was wrong when he started going on about how she was older than his usual type of girl, but so pretty and so fresh-faced and reached under his desk and pressed something that closed the door and blinds of his office. Then he started coming out with all that crap about trust and commitment and he asked her to take her top off. When she wouldn't do it the dirty old git became abusive, stood up, came up to her, put his face in hers, mouthing obscenities and stuck his hand between her legs.

That was her more than enough for Carrie. She kneed the scumbag in the balls. Hard. He fell to the floor, huffing and puffing in pain, and she aimed a quick kick to his face and was pleased to hear a satisfying crunch as his nose broke under the impact of her foot. From there she was right on her toes, round the back of the guy's desk, found the cheeky little button he'd pressed to lock the office door, pushed it, door opens, she jumps over the prostate figure of the revolting piece of filth and she's out of the office and out of the building.

Christ. What does she do now? She wants to punish the dirty, nasty pig: a knee in the balls and a busted nose isn't enough. She wants to screw him over, see him broken, destroyed, maybe even dead, not just for her but for all the other people that she is absolutely sure he's done this to before. But how? She knows the way fame and wealth work, knows there is no point going to the Old Bill or the media. Like that'll get her anywhere, this guy is far too rich and influential to be troubled by minor nonsense like police and press.

What on earth is she going to do? She needs to talk to someone about this, if not to get revenge then at least for her own sanity. Carrie pauses in her thoughts and stares down at her rapidly cooling mug of coffee-type drink. She looks up, and catches sight of an old tramp shuffling around the coffee bar, he's going from table to table, asking for money, getting nothing but refusals in the form of stunted shrugs and a half-mumbled "no, no." The tramp looks up from his latest unsuccessful prospect and his and Carrie's eyes meet. He is a ragged, dirty, rumpled man but, God, the eyes! To Carrie his eyes burn with an incredible intensity of intelligence and compassion. They are spellbinding. She can't understand why no one else has noticed them, why they should dismiss so readily a man who so obviously shines from his soul. The tramp smiles at Carrie, looking at her as though she's the exact person he's just popped into the coffee shop to meet. He heads straight for her table and in seconds, he is standing by her. He smells bad, of sweat and dirty clothes, but Carrie hardly notices, she is entranced by those eyes, waves of understanding and love seem to flow from them and she feels warm and comforted, as if someone has woven a net beneath her to catch her should she fall. She is convinced that she is in the company of an angel. A dirty, smelly, ragged angel, but an angel nevertheless. The tramp/angel opens his mouth and says to her to tell Johnny, Johnny will know what to do. Johnny will make everything right. And with that he turns away, walks out of the coffee bar and vanishes instantly into the crowds of Soho.

As if he had never been there.

Carrie is confused. She's calm and happy, her strange visitor has definitely improved her mood, but she's confused. Why did she think that the tramp was angel? After all, the idea of an angel disguised as a tramp walking through the streets of Soho is just silly…isn't it? But why did he know about Johnny? *How* did he know about Johnny? And why does she know as a matter of absolute certainty that she *is* going to tell Johnny exactly what that dirty, rich, famous, abusive piece of filth did to her?

'I Really Really Want It' is available now as an ebook and paperback:

Printed in Great Britain
by Amazon